PRAISE FOR

A THERAPEUTIC DEATH

BY J.B. STEVENS

"J.B. Stevens writes with compassion and nuance about ex-soldiers struggling to negotiate civilian life. His lyric prose is filled with sudden shifts that explode off the page."

—**Chris Offutt**, author of **The Killing Hills**

"A Therapeutic Death is a gathering of hard-hitting, fast-paced stories, littered with hardworn souls grasping for grace in deep and grim places. In other words, exactly what you want to see in a collection of stories unafraid of the dark."

—**Michael Farris Smith**, author of **Nick** and The **Fighter**

"Knockout prose in a fistful of words. I'll read anything J.B. Stevens writes."

—**Marc Cameron**, NYT Best Selling author of **Tom Clancy's Jack Ryan** thrillers

"J.B. Stevens writes whoop ass-fiction with the real-life experience to back up every word. You're in for a gut-punch of a read."

—**Mark Westmoreland**, author of **A Violent Gospel**

A THERAPEUTIC DEATH

VIOLENT SHORT STORIES

J.B. STEVENS

2022

A THERAPEUTIC DEATH: STORIES OF VIOLENCE
Text copyright © 2022 **J.B. STEVENS**

These stories first appeared in the following publications:
"A Good Man," Out of the Gutter Online; "A Red Flash," Story and Grit; "A Reliable Belt," Mistery Tribue; "A Wartime with Ramirez," Proud to Be Anthology; "Dead Camel," Short-Story.me; "Okefenokee Freedom," As You Were, Military Experience and Arts; "Overpower," The Nonconformist; "The Knife Angel," Punk Noir Magazine; "The Bunker," The Dead Mule School of Southern Literature; "The Exit," The Means at Hand; "The Hand Print," Mystery Tribune; "The Hostess Stand," New Pop Lit; "The Hustle," Punk Noir Magazine; "The Knowledge," Punk Noir Magazine; "The Lake," Mystery Tribune; "The Mask," Noir Nation; "The Missionary," Thriller Magazine; "The Orange Key," O Dark Thirty Literary Journal; "The Palm Grove," The Deadly Writers Patrol; "To Keep a Secret," Mystery Tribube

Published by Shotgun Honey Books

Shotgun Honey
215 Loma Road
Charleston, WV 25314
www.ShotgunHoney.com

Cover Design by Daniel Morgan.
Additional design by Bad Fido.

First Printing 2022.

ISBN-10: 1-956957-04-9
ISBN-13: 978-1-956957-04-4

9 8 7 6 5 4 3 2 1

For Erica and Claire.

CONTENTS

(STORIES)

A THERAPEUTIC DEATH

TO KEEP A SECRET

KEITH MET BARRY at the Waffle House near Cherokee, in Western North Carolina's Appalachian high-country. Inside, it smelled of frying bacon and Clapton's "River of Tears" played from hidden speakers. The two men hugged, sat, and ordered from a fleshy waitress with nicotine-stained fingers.

After she left, Barry talked. "Think any more about my plan?"

"It's not the right move," Keith said. "We aren't drug dealers."

"You owe me," Barry said.

"And how many times do I have to pay?"

Barry coughed. "As many as it fucking takes."

"I'm not a dealer."

"I'm not either. I just need money. You know what I'm doing for cash. I don't even like men. I hate myself."

Keith sipped the coffee—grounds assaulted his mouth. "Grow up. We all hate ourselves. Some of us are just better actors."

"Help me with this one sale," Barry said.

"I can't," Keith said. "I'm a father. A legitimate businessman."

The waitress returned with food. Barry bit the waffle. Syrup dripped in dense brown globs. "Father? Like you spend any time with your kid. You're a horrible dad."

Keith let the barb slide. "I feel like I'm paying for your drug habit. We need to get you off the smack."

Barry looked up from the food. "Get off? I'm never getting off. I can't let that shit come back into my mind. Fuck you for being so... normal. I can't just forget."

"I never forgot anything," Keith said.

"What you did," Barry said. "What I helped you do. That's international front-page shit. One call to CID and you're in Leavenworth for war-crimes."

Keith breathed deep, like the VA yoga teacher had taught him. Keith's mind skipped back. He felt the blood, sticky on his hands, and he heard the call-to-prayer, and he smelled the dust... He shoved the memory down and away. "It's just..."

Barry frowned. "What?"

"You're a junkie," Keith said.

"So?"

"I want to support you, not sell drugs."

"I got problems and need money." Barry started crying.

"PTSD is real. You're the victim." A good lie, Keith almost believed it.

"Damn straight," Barry said.

"We'll get you right," Keith said. "You were with me then. I'm with you now."

"With you? I was following you. You were my officer and I saw what you did."

"A decade ago. Maybe it's time to move on?"

"Fuck you."

Keith's chest ached. Barry was the best of them. A pure soul. And the war had taken that purity and soiled it and it was gone forever. "Here's the deal," Keith said. "I bought you a thick-as-hell coat." He touched the package next to him in the booth.

"And?"

"I'm getting you a room at the motel, tomorrow," Keith said.

Barry grunted. "Why tomorrow?"

"I need time to get cash from my safe. I can't get a motel room with my credit card."

"Why?"

"So my ex doesn't see the credit-card statement at the next alimony hearing and think I'm screwing whores in motel rooms."

Barry grinned. "Fucking whores in motel rooms... again."

"Touché," Keith said.

"Whatever. And after the hotel?"

"Get you in rehab. You kick the junk and you're on with my landscaping crew."

"I should be leading them, not on the squad," Barry said. "You owe me. My silence is your entire life."

"That's why I'm hooking you up," Keith said. "My everything depends on your silence."

"You better not forget that."

"The motel's near the lake. Meet me by the Cheoah Dam. Tomorrow. Two."

"That's in the middle of nowhere," Barry said.

"I don't want my ex, or her people, seeing us," Keith said. "They're up and down those hollers."

"The hell am I supposed to do tonight?"

"That's why I got this coat, to take care of you." Keith held out the jacket.

It was nice. Notch lapels, navy-blue, a touch of cashmere in the blend. Keith had bought it at some cheesy surplus store with "Fortunate Son" playing on repeat. The place was full of rednecks lying about their time *in the shit*. They all wanted to play tough guy. The real tough guys didn't have anything left to prove.

Barry stood. Keith followed. He ushered Barry into the

deep-blue embrace. It flowed and rippled down his reedy frame. The coat would take care of Barry. The coat would fix things. The coat was true.

Barry smiled. He ran his hands down the sleeves. "Thanks, brother."

They hugged. Barry felt like a deflated football with sticks inside. Heroin was evil.

Barry needed peace. Keith needed to end the torment.

The coat was the best way to help.

The next morning, at the dam, Keith looked out over the concrete, waiting for his friend. Keith stood against a low wall—a foot away from the edge. The river thundered behind him like a kid's nightmare-monster.

Barry walked out of the forest, looking strung-out, a meth-head John Rambo. Barry smiled and spoke. "We good?"

"Will be," Keith said. He waved Barry over.

Barry came. Keith didn't move.

They hugged.

Keith turned and pushed.

Barry fell and screamed and banged into the river. The splash echoed. The nightmare monster grabbed Barry and the rapids covered his head and the yelling stopped and it was calm.

The coat made swimming impossible. The coat did its job.

Keith thought of that kid bleeding out in the Baghdad sand. Barry had died that day, he just didn't realize it... Death took a while to catch up.

Barry never had a chance.

Keith dropped the yuppie-special fly-fishing-rod he'd stolen from the Asheville prick that turned Barry out. Barry's Asheville sugar-daddy.

When the Sheriff found the clues, it'd all be clear.

Western North Carolina had so many drownings... Keith wondered if anyone would even care. Barry was just another white-trash junkie vet from the holler, drowned in the middle of nowhere, strung out and alone.

Relief surged. Keith knew he'd done the right thing. It was time to get home. It was his weekend with the kid.

Keith turned and walked away.

A WELL-LIT TRAIL

DAVID SANTANA AMBLED along life's shadier paths, but only for luminous reasons. He did what was necessary to take care of the people who mattered—a righteous existence. Momma deserved the best. In his heart, David knew he was the good guy.

He sat in the parked car. Savannah's ancient redbrick buildings pushed in, claustrophobic. David didn't know if the omnipresent urine scent came from the clomping horses or the drunk revelers, but the fragrance made him optimistic, it smelled like opportunity.

He was halfway between sleep and consciousness when his navy Audi's rear door opened. The stench of booze slid in, riding on a self-assured young man.

David turned. The interloper was an in-shape, All-American, frat-boy looking kid. His cobalt fishing shirt matched his blue eyes. He wore too-brief khaki shorts and boat shoes.

David grimaced. "You can't just jump in my car."

"Sorry, Bro." The All-American waved his hands, palms up.

"Get out."

"I saw the purple light, I thought you were my ride-share guy."

David felt the frustration. "I'm a driver. Not your driver. You didn't order a ride from me. Use the app and I'll pick you up."

The passenger reached into his pocket. He pulled out three one-hundred-dollar bills.

David's eyes widened. That would take care of a lot of mom's prescriptions.

"Bro," the All-American said. "I need to get to Tybee Island."

"Bro," David said. "I don't care."

"I'll give you a hundred, cash."

David thought about it. The All-American seemed hammered. David could probably get two hundred, or even drive somewhere and roll the kid.

He shook his head. No, that wasn't necessary, take the easy cash. No one gets hurt, everyone wins. Plus, with David's criminal record there was no need to risk another strike.

"I'll drive, for a hundred fifty," David said.

"Deal."

David locked the doors, turned on some 90s R & B, and drove away.

The All-American tapped David's shoulder. "Is this that old Blackstreet song?"

"No Diggity," David said.

"No Doubt."

"Good taste. So, how'd you end up in Savannah? You don't look like you're from here."

David frowned. "I was born here."

"You Mexican?"

David decided that maybe he should rob the kid. "Cuban."

"Like *Scarface*."

David looked in the rear-view mirror. The passenger's eyes were wild, and he was grinding his teeth. "Anyone ever tell you you're racist?"

"Settle down, snowflake. *Scarface* was awesome."

They rode in awkward silence for a minute, but the kid couldn't keep his mouth shut. "How'd your people end up here?"

"Mom drove north trying to get away from Miami's crime."

"Single-mother?"

"Yeah."

"Rough."

"I'm betting you weren't raised by a single mom."

"Good guess."

The passenger snorted. David looked in the rear-view mirror, the kid rubbed his nose.

"Your mom came to Savannah for safety? That seems dumb," the passenger said.

"It's worked out so far," David said.

David watched the All-American produce a baggie of white powder, pull out a key, and do a bump.

David loved cocaine, but not the consequences of having it around. "You doing blow in my car?"

"Chill, it's no big deal." The passenger flashed a perfect-toothed half smile.

"All right, blondie." David pulled over. "Get out."

"Not cool." The All-American frowned. "How about I give you two hundred and we call it even?"

"Don't be ridiculous. I'm not risking a charge for you."

The All-American looked like he might cry. "I'll give you three hundred."

"And the coke?"

"What about it?"

"I want it all."

"What? No!"

David hit the lock button. "Fine, I'll drive us to the police station."

The kid handed him the bag. "You suck."

"Smart," David said. "Now give me your key." He did a bump, slipped the bag in his pocket, and handed back the key.

The All-American finally went silent. At the parking lot, he handed over the three hundred-dollar bills and got out, wordless.

David smiled, a successful trip.

A few hours and a few fares later, on his way home, David saw the blue lights. He thought of the coke in his pocket and started to sweat. He pulled over. The cops ordered him out, cuffed him, and searched him. They found the drugs and took him into custody.

David sat in the cold, antiseptic-scented, interview room, secured to a stainless-steel table. He felt trapped and he remembered the burning vehicle in Baghdad. Luckily, an AC turned on, and the cold air pulled him back to reality.

A guy in a wrinkled short-sleeve button-down sauntered in. He oozed false confidence and self-doubt.

"My name is Detective Dustin Michael. Did the arresting officer read you your Miranda rights, and did you understand them?"

"Yes."

"Good. We're here to talk about the Thunderbird Motel."

David felt relieved. This was a misunderstanding. He would get a possession charge and lose the three hundred dollars, but that was it.

"Sorry, Detective," David said. "I haven't been there in weeks."

Dustin sighed. "This goes much better if you tell the truth."

"I am."

"You don't remember me?"

"No."

"I snagged you on a breaking and entering."

"That should have been trespassing," David said.

"You were looking for opiates," Dustin said.

"I was exploring an abandoned building... Just like I told the Judge."

"I know the real you. Tell the truth."

"No idea what you're getting at."

Dustin sighed and tented his fingers on the table. "Tell me about the shooting."

David felt a twitch in his right eye. "Huh?"

"D-Fresh."

Dave's throat tightened. "What?"

Dustin leaned in. "You have a beef with the Carver Crips?"

"I don't—"

"Tell me it was an accident..."

"But I didn't—"

Dustin leaned back. "You're a good guy and got caught in an impossible situation... You're the real victim."

"I have no idea what you are talking about."

The detective got red faced and left. Ten minutes later Dustin returned. He had three clear evidence bags. One held an iPhone, not David's. Another secured the All-American's coke-key. The third bag had the one-hundred-dollar bills.

Dustin pushed the baggies towards David. "What about these?"

"Some frat-boy hired me for a ride," David said. "That's his key and money. I've never seen the phone."

The detective looked down and pinched the bridge of his nose. "Do I look like an idiot?"

"No."

"This cash was in your pocket."

"The pay for the ride. I drive for a service."

"That means there's a record in an app?"

David swallowed. "Well... no... he hopped in, offered cash."

"Convenient. So, this time there is no record."

"Right."

Dustin gestured at the bags. "And that phantom frat-boy left this."

"Correct."

"That'll hold up well in court."

David's heart pounded. He thought about mom. He thought about his dog. "Court?"

Dustin leaned back. "You handle any of this?"

"Key and cash, not the phone, why?"

"Foundation for the DNA test."

David's mouth went dry. "That doesn't mean anything."

"Your DNA is on two pieces of evidence. The third was under your seat. Supposedly, given to you by an unnamed kid you drove. But there is no record, even though everything is through the app."

"Exactly."

"Cut the crap," Dustin said. "Is this D-Fresh's cocaine?"

"Who?"

The detective sighed. "Is there coke in your bloodstream?"

"Yes, but I can explain that."

The detective dropped his head and rubbed his temples. He looked like a man with two divorces under his belt, marching towards number three.

"D-Fresh came at you," Dustin said. "Self-defense. You did what you had to do…"

"I have no idea what you're talking about," David said.

"The evidence is overwhelming."

"Evidence of what?"

"The position of the body." Dustin shook his head. "So many gunshots. It shocks the conscience. Why disrespect a corpse? Was this personal?"

"I've no idea what you're talking about."

The detective looked up with tired eyes. "You murdered D-Fresh."

David vomited on the steel table.

The Detective jumped away and stomped out of the room, leaving David chained in his own sick.

Ten minutes later, the public defender arrived, smiling with little yellow teeth. His suit fit like a prom rental tux and his shoes featured rubber soles. David knew, good lawyers' shoes were all leather.

Half-way into the room, the lawyer frowned. "What's that smell?"

"I puked," David said.

"They left you in here?"

David didn't answer as the question was stupid. The lawyer pounded on the door and a uniformed cop answered.

"We need a new room," the lawyer said.

The cop frowned. "What's wrong with this one?"

"Smells like vomit."

"Probably cause that idiot vomited."

"Get us a new room."

The fat cop took his time putting on black latex gloves. He unlocked the cuffs with chubby, unsure fingers. The three went into the space next door, a mirror image of the last. However, this one was puke-free. The cop locked David down and left.

The lawyer took a seat.

David rested his head on the cool metal. "Whatever happens, I don't want to put my mother through a trial."

"I would advise against a trial. At this point, the evidence is airtight," rubber-soles said.

"What can we do?"

"Act like we're fighting."

"Act?"

"I mean, we really fight, of course, but we need to take a plea as soon as they put something good on the table."

"But I'm innocent."

The lawyer started laughing. "Course you are, and no one cares. We'll have your arraignment tomorrow." The lawyer slid a representation agreement across the table. David signed it with a stubby stab-proof pencil.

The lawyer stood. "Keep your mouth shut. If you're innocent, the truth will come out."

David sighed, any lawyer that says "if you're innocent" was just after billable hours.

After the papers were signed, and the lawyer left, the fat cop came back in. "Let's go to holding."

David strolled down the jail corridor. All the lights were burnt out.

THE HOSTESS STAND

DANH TRAN NEVER planned to be a restaurateur. His parents moved from Hanoi to L.A. when Dan was four. Mom was trying to get away from the war. Dad was trying to forget the pain. Neither got over the trauma. After the riots they moved to Atlanta. It was a good choice, their restaurant was doing well.

Atlanta's residents were nice, they welcomed the Trans. Growing up, he told everyone to call him "Dan" and that he was from Alabama. Danh watched the *Dukes of Hazzard* nightly to perfect his fake southern accent. It felt a little slimy, lying for convenience, but he got used to it. It was for the best. Sometimes you had to play along to get along.

The Crazy Chicken Café was nobody's idea of fine dining. Stupid décor and non-offensive pop music were the themes, but Dan didn't mind. The generic soul food buffet was a cash cow, and he loved the smell of fried chicken.

His dad, Hung, wanted him to follow the family tradition and become a doctor, or an accountant like his brother, or an orthodontist like his sister. But Dan didn't care for school. Besides, Dan was still Hung's favorite.

After a few years, when the place started turning a healthy profit, he realized he enjoyed owning a restaurant. It was nice to make good money. He was able to donate thousands of dollars a year to the Buddhist temple on Shallowford Road. He'd even paid for an outreach program back in Vietnam. The charity made him feel good.

His wife, Leslie, did not support his philanthropic work. She was the Crazy Chicken's first hostess, and current new-employee trainer. Every staff member went through Leslie before they got to Dan.

When he knocked Leslie up, they got married. She was nineteen and blonde and vibrant. Dan was thirty-seven and a smoker.

Now Leslie stayed at home, like she wanted, barefoot and pregnant. She gave Dan grief about working long hours. She always smelled his clothes for perfume, but she never complained about the money.

That's how it was in America. You could do what you wanted, if you had the cash. The people at the temple didn't love his lifestyle, but they accepted his checks. Leslie didn't care for his extracurricular activities, but she still drove the BMW and ate brunch at the country club. Let them complain. They needed him. He was a good man, and he knew it.

He got to the restaurant around dinner on Tuesday. He felt good. The place smelled like fried chicken and his mouth watered. The air-conditioning was crisp, a nice change from outside. When he saw Crystal's face the mood shifted.

Dan liked Crystal. Her shorts where short and her shirt was tight. She was a great hostess. She looked like the kind of girl an out of shape, middle-aged guy had no business sleeping with. But she was exactly the kind of girl a well-off businessman slept with… it was good to be the boss.

He smiled and gave her a hug. "What's up?

That's when the mascara ran.

Dan put his arm around her shoulder. She smelled like strawberry lotion. He breathed deep. "Come to the office."

They walked to the back. He felt a stirring, being alone with her, but forced himself to hold off. No one liked to have a crying woman. "Tell me what's going on."

"I'm late," Crystal said. The tears evolved to racked sobs.

Dan's chest exploded. "What do you mean?"

"What the fuck do you think I mean?"

Visions of divorce lawyers and custody battles and alimony and two women drawing child support danced through his head. Dan wanted to come on strong but knew that it was the wrong move. Eighteen-year-olds are delicate and emotional. He had to slow play it.

"Tell me what you're feeling," Dan said.

Crystal exploded. She had the kind of voice a guy from New York thinks a southern woman should have. She was always a talker. She dove in.

For twenty minutes she spoke about her momma, her daddy—the Baptist minister, her plan to be a teacher, her time in Sunday school, and the guilt of being the other woman. Her life was over, and she wanted to die.

Teenagers were so dramatic.

Dan held her and stroked her blonde hair and told her it would all be ok. She sat in his lap and cried on his shoulder. He felt the familiar pull. He cupped her backside. She said no and he stopped.

The rest of the day was a haze. When he got home, Leslie asked him what was wrong. He played it off as an issue with expired okra. He had a drink and then another. They made love and he forgot for a while.

The next few weeks were a mist. Crystal wanted him to go to the Doctor's appointments. He refused, saying he had to stay at the restaurant. He gave her cash to pay. Leslie kept asking what was going on, he kept blaming restaurant supplier issues.

On the morning of the fourth week, he called Crystal to his office. The decision hurt, but it was the right thing.

"I think we need to consider… All of our options," Dan said.

Crystal looked up, red and wet. Her stomach was starting to grow. George Michael's "Faith" played on the sound system.

"What do you mean?"

"There's a Planned Parenthood in East Atlanta. I can take you. It's for the best."

Crystal exploded. Dan held her and they talked. She was a Christian and couldn't do it. After an hour, she agreed. He felt sad but knew it was the right move.

She called him the following Wednesday, after lunch. She was upset.

"It's done."

"Are you ok?"

"No. Can you give me four hundred dollars?"

Dan heard the pain in her voice. "Come over to the restaurant."

They talked and cried. Eventually, Crystal told him she was leaving town, going to California. She was starting Art school and getting away from the bullshit.

She held up her phone. The tuition page for San Diego State's art program was there.

"What's this?"

"This is how much I need. Plus, enough for food and the dorms for a year."

"I can't afford this."

Crystal's face went hard. "You don't have a choice. I'll tell your wife everything."

It hit Dan like a truck. Dan felt the rage but then the calm.

She was right, there was nothing else to do. It's better to accept these things.

"Give me a day," Dan said.

The bank manager was kind. After Dan showed him the title for the Mercedes, they stroked a check for forty grand. He cashed it and called Crystal.

They met in Dan's office. He gave her the money. He tried to kiss her, but her face was a mask of disgust. She left and it was over, and he felt relief.

He called the temple and made a large donation. Dan liked to balance the good with the bad.

It was three weeks later when the new hostess, Tiffany, called him. Dan liked Tiffany. She was fit.

"Some guy is here, he said he needs to see you."

Dan went to the front desk. The process server was business-like. Dan was a bit disappointed the guy didn't say "You got served!" but that must only be in the movies.

The divorce papers were clear. Leslie wanted half of everything. Dan googled the name of Leslie's lawyer. The attorney was a beast.

When Dan got home the place was empty. Leslie took everything, even his recliner. She hated the recliner—taking it seemed petty.

In the middle of the floor was a photo of Leslie and Crystal from a training day at the restaurant. They were sitting on his desk smiling. Underneath was a note in Leslie's handwriting.

"Thanks for paying for my divorce lawyer. Go fuck yourself."

Dan was angry, but it passed. He smiled. Leslie was too sharp to stay barefoot and pregnant.

He sat on the floor, looked at the picture, and wondered what Tiffany was doing after work.

THE ORANGE KEY

THE SLAP LANDED clean. Clinton heard it echo off the cinder block walls.

"I think I'm going to shit myself," Clinton said as he tried to escape.

"You're such a little bitch," Alec said, laughing.

Sweat dripped off Alec's chin and into Clinton's eyes. Clinton realized it was becoming hard to breathe. Slowly he snaked his right hand to Alec's left hip and right elbow into Alec's stomach.

Clinton hooked his left arm over the back of Alec's head. Pulling down with the left while pushing up with the right and arching his back, Clinton rolled Alec over.

Clinton put his right knee on Alec's chest and kept his left foot wide for balance. While kneeling on Alec's chest Clinton punched him hard, in the face, twice.

Alec yelled, "TAP!"

Clinton shifted off his friend. Pushing wet brown hair behind a pale, mangled ear he thought about how much the kid had improved.

Alec possessed real talent. He could go far in the MMA world… if he stayed focused.

"I thought you had me for a second," Clinton said.

"Thought so too, but then I was on my back, and you punched me in the face."

"That's why I'm the coach."

Alec touched his lip and examined the red liquid. "This my blood or yours?"

"You know the answer."

"It's always my blood."

"With how ugly you are it can only improve the situation."

"Your mom seems to like my situation."

Clinton threw a jab. The fist caught Alec squarely on his bare chest. Alec coughed and rolled backwards. They both laughed.

Clinton smiled. "Yo-momma jokes?"

"They're classics for a reason."

"Anyway, about that position, you're getting better. Two years ago you couldn't last thirty seconds."

"When'll I be ready?" Alec adjusted the protective cup under the black spandex.

"When do I think you'll be ready to fight, or when do I think a promoter will be ready to pay you to get in the cage?"

"Both. I need money, bad. My family is struggling, and I'd do just about anything for cash."

"Here's the thing, you got a good back story, no criminal record, no tattoos, weren't born with a silver spoon in your mouth, hard upbringing, taking care of your mom and little brother, your dad leaving when you were a baby, all that crap."

"Crap?"

You're still approachable and good-looking. A promoter would take you on in a second, but...

"But?"

"They'll throw you to the wolves."

"Yea?"

"We need to get you seasoned. Then we start looking at fights, but the right fights."

"What do you mean?"

"Challenges that are reasonable. We don't want cans that you will run through, but we also don't want to throw you in with the sharks."

"Take it slow?"

"Measured, get you to 5-0. Then get you a bigger fight. You win and you're ready for the big show."

"UFC?"

"Win there and you can make real money."

"Seems doable."

"It'll take a few years, but if we do it right, sky's the limit."

"My Georgia Power bill won't wait 5 years. A good story doesn't mean shit without electricity."

"Bills don't wait, but brain damage is forever."

"Ha."

"You want to stay with me, you have to do it the right way. And I'm the only legit trainer willing to do it for free."

"I guess we're stuck together."

Alec sighed and walked to the showers.

Clinton took out the mop and began his nightly cleaning ritual. The bleach smelled strongly.

Clinton was wiping down a heavy bag when he heard a scream from behind the building. "Coach, I need you now!"

Running outside, he saw Alec standing in the trash-scented alley. Next to a green dumpster, slumped against the damp red-brick wall, was a man. His hair was dark and wavy, and his olive-skinned face was clean-shaven. A gold necklace around his neck said "Bruno" in large letters. He wore a well-tailored grey suit, open collared white shirt, polished black loafers, and a matching black belt. The belt's buckle was a golden alligator. There was a tan leather duffel bag on the ground. Bruno was covered in blood.

Clinton's heart started pounding. "What the hell, Alec?"

"He was like this when I got here. What the fuck! The police are going to think I did this."

"Settle down, as long as you didn't touch him, you're fine."

"I take care of my whole family. I can't deal with this shit!" Alec said.

"You've done nothing wrong, and you have nothing to worry about. We're going to call the cops and get this straightened out."

"Are there any cameras out here?"

"No," Clinton said. "It's a dirty alley behind a shitty building, why would there be cameras? Relax, you're good. You watch those CSI shows, right? None of your DNA's on this guy. None of your hair's on this guy. Who-ever fucked him up, that DNA will be all over the place."

"Should we look for a wallet or something? Do you know who this dude is?"

"I think we shouldn't touch shit, we should just call the cops."

"All right, let me go grab my cell phone."

Alec turned and walked towards the gym's open door. Clinton remained with the body. He noticed the duffel bag was unzipped.

"Alec, hold on, what's inside the bag?"

"I don't give a shit. Let's just call the cops. The less we deal with this headache the better."

"It looks like cash," Clinton said.

"Who gives a… wait… how much cash?"

"How much does it take to fill a duffel bag with 100-dollar bills?"

"Enough to think twice. What do we do now?"

"How the fuck am I supposed to know?"

"We should call the cops. This is serious shit. Who would kill a guy and leave that much money?"

Clinton looked up and down the alley. He didn't see anyone.

"No one saw shit. It will be a headache proving we didn't do this. But I am sure that the CSI crap will be on our side." Clinton said.

"No one saw shit…" Alec said.

"I know, I just told you that."

"If there aren't any cameras… That means no one except me, you, and Bruno know about this money."

"Who gives a fuck?"

"I work at fucking Burger King. I know your gym doesn't make shit for profit."

"Yea, and if we screw around with this," Clinton waved at the bag. "We make ourselves suspects in a murder."

"I know," Alec said. "We could also pay rent and buy groceries. The dead guy doesn't need it. I could buy a car for my mom and pay for a nice apartment in a good school district for my brother. I don't want my brother to experience the same crap as me. The cash would solve a lot of problems for both of us. We don't want it sitting in some evidence room, right? What good would it do? And if it is some asshole's drug money then we are doing the right thing by keeping it."

Clinton realized Alec was making a lot of sense. Neither had a bright future. Getting punched in the face, or teaching people how to punch faces, didn't have a retirement plan.

"I bet some dirty cop will probably keep it anyway," Clinton said.

"If not a dirty cop," Alec said, "the government will keep it. Probably use it to pay for a park bench in a rich suburb."

"We could hold it for a minute, see if someone comes around, asking about it."

"We really wouldn't be doing anything wrong."

"We would be doing a good thing."

"Making sure this money does something positive. You're already, basically, running a charity with how little your gym earns."

"You are making a lot of sense."

"Think about it, you help people and never ask for anything in return," Alec said. "You deserve this money. Life hasn't given me shit. I deserve a boost. Maybe this is the chance we both need."

"Are you sure this is the right thing?"

"I am," Clinton said. "It would be the right thing for us to keep it."

"Yea, but what do we do with this body? What do we do with the cash while we wait?"

"I think we just leave the body. No one knows we were here, our priority's the money."

"The bus station over on Oglethorpe Avenue, it is the most anonymous place in the world."

"We could get a locker at the station, put the bag in there, then come back and call the cops and report the body."

"Make sense."

They marched the six blocks to the bus station. Alec carried the bag. Clinton kept an eye out for trouble.

They entered the bus station. It smelled like industrial cleaning products and unwashed travelers. A woman was having a fight on speaker phone, her man was cheating. They found an empty locker, 1789, put in their duffel bag, and took the small orange-tipped key. Clinton realized they had crossed a line, but there was no turning back now.

Alec turned to Clinton. "What next?"

"We call the cops and report the dead guy," Clinton said. "If no one comes calling after a few months we count it and split it. But we need to be calm and stay cool. If we fuck this up, we're going down for murder. If we do this right, we're rich."

"Who keeps the key?"

"We have to trust each other. I trust you. You can keep it. But remember, if we fuck this up… It's death penalty type shit."

Clinton watched as Alec took a red shoelace out of his black Vans. He put the orange key onto the lace, tied a knot, and then put the lace around his neck.

"Let's go back to the gym and call the cops. We tell the whole truth, everything 100% legit. We just leave out the duffel bag and bus station. Other than that, the whole truth, no lies, no fuck ups." Clinton said as he turned and started walking.

Clinton took them back by a slightly different route, to make sure no one saw them twice and remembered their passing. They arrived at the gym, cut through the inside, went to the alley, and approached the body. The dead man lay undisturbed. Clinton got his mind ready to call the cops, mentally rehearsing what he was going to say.

As he was preparing to dial, he sensed movement from behind. Turning, he saw a fist clutching a knife coming at him in a long overhead arc. His mind switched from scared witness to fighter. Time slowed, his years of training kicked in.

The attacker was a well-dressed and dark-haired man. Clinton reached up with his left arm. He took a small step towards the attacker and caught the forearm, stopping the arc of the knife. At the same time, he struck his opponent in the face with a right elbow. He grasped the left wrist and over hooked the neck.

Clinton drove his hips through to the attacker's right side. Dropping his weight low and back he exploded up while turning to his left, a textbook perfect hip throw. The attacker's feet arced overhead, and he slammed into the pavement. The impact was loud. The knife fell out of the attacker's hand and clattered to the ground.

Clinton dropped his right knee onto the attacker's chest. He heard the crunch of broken ribs. Placing his left foot out wide for balance, he punched the attacker twice in the face, hard. The attacker went limp, probably knocked out, but maybe dead, Clinton didn't care. He stood and turned, looking for other opponents. There was no one there but Alec.

As Clinton gathered his thoughts, he felt a burning sensation in his side. What the fuck was that? Looking down he saw blood. It became hard to breathe and the air smelled metallic. Why weren't his lungs working?

Alec held a knife. The same knife the attacker had been holding.

"I am so sorry." Alec looked down. Tears rolled down his cheeks. "The money, I can't share it. I need it all. I am sorry."

Clinton's mind started burning... What the fuck, what the fuck, what the fuck, the phrase cycled over and over. "We're friends?"

"I had to... for my family."

Alec reached down to take out his other red shoelace. He tied the attacker's wrists and gently wrapped an unconscious hand around the bloody knife. Taking off his grey sweatshirt, he soaked up some of Clinton's blood. He covered the knocked-out man in red, then placed the sweatshirt over Clinton's wound.

Alec waited until Clinton didn't have a pulse for a full five minutes. He wiped away the tears and swallowed his guilt. He took out his phone and dialed 911.

As it rang, he rehearsed what he would say. When a 911 operator picked up, he was ready. "Hello? Hello? O God! I need the police! Someone just stabbed my coach. There is a dead body out here. What the fuck! I need the police now! I have no idea what the hell is going on. We are at Unity Fighting Club. Please hurry. O God, please hurry!"

He fingered the orange key and waited for the cops.

THE
HANDPRINT

HAMBURG'S PORT HOUSED thousands of shipping containers. Finding a peaceful spot was easy. The space was dark, and sound echoed.

Sam ignored the piss. The feces were harder, but Sam was a professional. He checked the zip-ties, still good. He got the smelling salts and gave Hans a whiff.

Blue eyes opened.

"We aren't done."

Sam grabbed blonde hair. He scalped the kid and dropped the mess in Hans's naked lap. Hans screamed.

"Now it won't block your view."

Hans cried for a long time. He started puking again. Sam hooked up the seventh IV bag.

"I don't know the room in the photo," Hans said. His English was good, only a slight accent. "I have no idea what you're talking about."

"Your text messages disagree," Sam said.

"Fake. Planted."

"Stop the denials. Look at the picture. The room. The handprint."

"No."

Sam got out the bolt cutter and cut off the third toe on Han's right foot.

"Seven left."

Hans wept, then talked.

"We did it. I remember the little windows. I was high, an accident. I'm sorry."

"Clarity makes my boss happy. Thank you."

Sam had given the kid a lot of meth. The drugs put off an ammonia smell.

Sam removed all ten fingers and the remaining toes. He hooked up a fresh IV bag in each arm.

"You should bleed out, but I gave you so many bags… you could last a long time, but that's a lot of trauma. I don't know. Whatever, you shouldn't have raped my boss's daughter."

As ordered, Sam stuffed the fingers and toes into the kid's mouth and taped it shut. He left the container, locked it, and went to the airport.

Sam was back in Phoenix by morning. His wife made eggs. He ate with his son. It was the American Dream.

OVERPOWER

I DIDN'T KNOW banks were still open, my lucky day. Breathing is so damn hard. I see the mop bucket and bleach bottle, I can't smell them, but I remember.

Everything is out-of-focus. I need air.

"Give me the fucking money."

She sounds like a hurricane and overpowers the tasteless instrumental pop.

"Stop crying. Fuck, I don't want to hurt you, I don't want to hurt anyone, fuck."

Everyone is wearing masks and gloves… it makes this part easier, cleaner.

"Just the register. Fast, fast, fast."

Bartenders don't get paid if they don't work.

Outside—in the rust bucket Honda Civic I got off that drunk—the streets are empty, no good, Asheville is a small town. If the teller calls the cops I'm done.

The dirt bike is in the culvert next to the public hospital. It is easy to blend in. So much death. The parking lot smells like piss and there is a bum sleeping on the splintered asphalt.

He isn't snoring and his lungs sound good, I wish I could fucking breath. I wish I had good lungs, need to lay off the skunk. How does this bum live next to a fucking den of infection and I get it?

I know I'm dying. I know I have it. I know. Whatever, death, jail, at least Camille gets some money.

I love her.

I wish I would just die already.

If I don't get caught, I'm doing the same shitty thing tomorrow.

I wish I would just die, but I remember.

THE KNOWLEDGE

THE VFW WAS mostly empty.

Duke sighed. "It's never easy."

"It's a sure thing," Zeke said.

"Last 'sure thing'...wasn't."

"Cops never got us."

"Only 'cause Smitty was on patrol and let us slide."

"Knowledge of war crimes makes a great get-out-of-jail-free card."

"You play that one too much. Where'd you get tonight's tip?"

"Smitty."

Duke nodded.

"Self-storage on Benedict Arnold Drive," Zeke said. "5 p.m. Bring zip-ties."

"Or?"

"Your secrets end up on Wikileaks."

Duke missed the clarity of war.

Smitty pulled out the heroin. "ODing is like riding a summer-breeze."

Zeke struggled against the zip-ties. They held.

A RELIABLE BELT

VAGNER DOS SANTOS didn't want to kill the guard. He had no choice. The half-way house was not secure, only one person kept them in. The cheap owners needed to invest in manpower. There are bad people in the world. He was not one of them. Vagner knew it wasn't his fault.

The watchman walked by Vagner's bunk after midnight. Snores and coughs filled the calm. The place smelled the way a warehouse full of a hundred convicts should smell. The moist funk got in your mouth and permeated your skin.

The guard was on his cell phone swiping right. Americans loved technology. Vagner missed Brazil, it was a simpler place. The people were more consistent.

Vagner needed to get home. He wanted to help his family. He'd only moved to Utah to make money for them. Vagner didn't like the snow, or the fake religious people, or the weird food, but he managed.

The Mormon Church helped. Vagner tried to stay true to his religion. He never did anything wrong that wasn't one-hundred-percent necessary. He even wore the prescribed modest undergarments, a challenge for a person raised in the Brazilian *sunga* speedo. But Vagner was happy to do it. It was joyful to live in the glory of one's faith.

Vagner grabbed his braided leather belt. His *porra* father made the strap from the skin of horses they'd killed on their *fazenda*. Vagner's dad beat the family with it. Vagner took it the day the abuse ended.

The fat American's back was turned. Vagner looped the belt around the neck. Vagner was tall for a Brazilian, the same height as the big gringo. He pulled close. The American smelled like McDonald's.

The man clawed at Vagner's face. Vagner saw grease under the yellow fingernails. Vagner tucked his head between the shoulder blades. The struggle was short. The guard was out of shape and didn't fight hard.

After the movement stopped Vagner held the belt to make sure the job was done. He put it back in his faded jeans and listened. Even snoring, no one woke up.

Vagner went through the dead man's pockets. He grabbed cash, car keys, and the housing facility's magnetic door lock.

He dragged the flabby body to the linen closet. He muscled it to the back and covered it with sheets.

Vagner went to his locker and put on a clean pink polo shirt. He liked pink, it made him seem gentle. He used the card to go outside. Vagner found the guard's vehicle, an old white truck. It was large and boxy. American's loved big cars.

Vagner said a prayer for the dead man. He did not like to hurt people. If he could make it to Mexico, then he could get a new identity and fly back to Brazil. He just had to get from Salt Lake City to the border. He didn't know the way, but he knew to head south.

The sun broke over the snow-topped Wasatch Mountains. The high desert pushed in around him. The day was sunny and clear. It was good to be free. He could go home, work, help mom.

He was a quarter of the way to Las Vegas when the blue

lights came. He looked at his speedometer. Vagner was going too fast. Stupid. He had no driver's license, only the dead guy's cash.

The officer came up. He looked fresh, clean. He was alone.

"Morning," the cop said. The name tag said Young. "You were going a bit quick. License, registration, proof of insurance please."

Vagner knew his heart should be pounding, but it wasn't. Vagner smelled Young's aftershave and looked at the dusty police car and stared at the cop. It was nice to be free. Vagner adjusted his belt.

"Sure," Vagner said. "Let me grab it."

Vagner leaned to the glove compartment, grabbed the stack of papers, and turned back. Vagner smiled. The prison dentist did good work. His lean dark features and exotic look got strong reactions in Utah.

Young smiled. Vagner knew right then. He put the papers on the center seat next to him. Young wasn't wearing a wedding ring.

"You look familiar," Vagner said. "Have I seen you before?"

Young's blue eyes widened. He brushed blonde hair behind a pale ear and looked at his shoes for a moment.

"No," Young said. "I don't think so. Where are you from?"

"Not from around here, do you know Brazil?"

Young's eyebrows shot up.

"*Eu sei,*" Young said. "*Voce?*"

"*Sim,*" Vagner said. "*Eu estou brasileiro.*"

"Small world. I did my mission in Recife."

"Mormon mission?"

"Yes."

"I'm a Latter-day Saint as well, brother. I'm from Rio."

"*Um carioca.*"

"*Sim.*"

"Good stuff. Anyway… your license. I'll get you on your way fast… Maybe we can talk later… About Brazil."

"I'd like that."

Vagner smiled and winked. Young blushed. Young put his hand on the windowsill. Vagner put his on top. The kid jumped, but relaxed. Both left their hands in place.

"Your license…"

Vagner sighed. "Of course." He shifted to grab the papers. He turned back and threw them in Young's face.

Young bent left. Vagner threw the door open. It slammed into Young's knees.

Young rolled back and settled on his stomach. He moved his left hand to the hip. Vagner recognized the taser.

The electric weapon came up. Vagner stepped right. Young reached his hand to the radio microphone.

Vagner ran over and kicked Young in the face. Young screamed and tried to get up. Vagner kicked him three more times in the head. Young stopped trying to get up.

Vagner looked up and down on the highway. They were alone. Vagner thought about the dash and body cameras but realized it probably uploaded to the cloud somewhere. It was too late now.

Vagner wrapped the braided horsehide belt around Young's neck. He pulled. After a minute the breathing stopped. He held it for a beat longer.

Why did these people keep making him do this? He hated hurting others… Why couldn't they just leave him alone?

Vagner grabbed the cop's key. He moved the police car to the road's shoulder and put Young in the front seat. It looked like any officer checking for speeders.

Vagner put the belt back on. The belt was trustworthy, strong. He got back in the pickup and headed south. He figured he could be at the border by morning.

He stopped at a little roadside motel after sundown. It was low-slung and painted orange. He paid cash and went to his room. It was full of polyester fabrics and re-production paintings. Everything in the United States was fake.

He went to sleep thinking about the beach in Rio, acai, his mom's rice and beans.

Vagner woke with a start. He didn't know why, but he was blind, and his ears rang.

Many hands touched him. They started hitting. He felt the shock of the Taser. Soon the world was pain.

"Kill a fucking cop, you piece of shit? He was my battle buddy in Iraq. We made it through hell so you could smoke him? I owe him my God-Damned life."

Something hit his head, hard, and he went away.

Vagner woke up in a small damp place. It was grey and paint chips floated from the ceiling and it smelled like cleaning products. He heard coughing and an air-conditioner humming.

A big, pale, blonde man sat across from him. He was flushed and sweaty with bloodshot eyes.

"My name is Brigham Young," the man said. "I'm the Sheriff. First thing we do, after every murder, is check the cheaper motels. With your picture from the dash-cam... it didn't take long."

Young looked up. Vagner followed. The braided leather belt was tied around a pipe. It hung, a loop at the end.

Vagner knew he should feel afraid, but he didn't. He tried to move his arms, but they were bound. He looked down.

Nephi punched him in the face. Stars flashed and Vagner got dizzy. Nephi picked him up, looped the belt around Vanger's neck, and lowered the weight.

Nephi punched him in the testicles.

The world faded. Vagner fought against the restraints, but they didn't give.

Vagner felt horsehide on his neck.

The darkness washed over him.

THE ANGEL

THE KNIFE ANGEL brought tourists. A hundred thousand blades surrendered and turned into a sculpture. The piece sucked joy, a black hole, clouding everything nearby. Back home in Savannah everyone had guns. Here in Britain, it was knives. Same problem, different tool.

Each visitor was an opportunity. Billy made the most of it. When he left Georgia to go to Hull York Medical School his family was ecstatic. Every American mom wants to tell the book club her son's a doctor.

He met Sarah at orientation, first day. She liked his American accent. She said he reminded her of Johnny Depp.

Billy didn't know what Sarah found appealing. Girls never liked him. He was awkward.

After two months of studying together he asked Sarah out. He was shocked when she said yes. She was out of his league. They went for fish and chips because Billy didn't know any better.

The first three months were the best of his life.

In the spring Sarah got her wisdom teeth out. The doctor cut a prescription for Percocet. She liked it. After a few weeks, she lost weight. After a few months, her skin went translucent.

By fall Sarah was injecting cheap black tar heroin.

At first, he fought. Then he joined. They were in love and should be tighter.

The University kicked them out in spring. It was a warm day, smelled like flowers.

They lived in an empty redbrick building. Back home, someone would have turned it into lofts. Made money. Here it disintegrated into nothing.

Billy's parents thought he was still in school. The money they sent wasn't enough.

England is an island, import costs are through the roof.

Billy needed to pay for Sarah's rehab. Jamming people up to earn money wasn't fun, but if he didn't get her in-patient treatment soon, she was going to kill herself.

He'd already caught her on the corner twice, earning money her way. Sarah promised she would stop. It broke Billy's soul.

Billy usually waited for drunks outside Admiral Casino, lots of cash, easy targets. The casino was halfway between the aquarium and the Knife Angel over at Queens Gardens.

Sarah was dope sick the day Billy went to see the Angel when it first came to town.

The sun was rising, and Billy was outside the Admiral. He noticed the jacket first. It was tan cashmere and fit perfectly, custom made. Billy checked the watch, Omega, and the shoes, oxblood calfskin. Money for sure.

Billy fell in behind.

The guy took a right on Princes Dock towards the Angel.

He could rob the guy by the roundabout and disappear into the alleyways. The Omega made it worth the risk. The wallet was a bonus.

The alley smelled like puke and he saw a used needle. Fucking junkies. He changed to a hoody and sunglasses so the cameras couldn't catch his face.

He caught up one street over. The guy's dark hair was slick, and he smelled like expensive cologne, and had that erect military-man posture. He had one earphone in. Billy made out the sound of 80's pop music… Sting.

"Hey," Billy said. "Got a cigarette?"

The guy turned. Disgust flashed. The guy should show some respect. A year ago, Billy was a medical student.

"American?"

"Yea," Billy said. "British?"

"Yes. I don't smoke."

"Maybe I could get some cash?"

Billy didn't see any cameras, and no one was around.

"Sorry. Only got plastic."

Billy pulled the knife.

"How about you give me the wallet and watch."

Two hands went up.

"You can have it all. No problems."

Billy felt tired. He hoped Sarah was ok. There was no dope at home.

"What size shoe you wear?"

"Eleven."

"Give me the shoes."

The guy kneeled, started untying. He took off the right, then left, and stood.

Billy shifted the knife to his off hand. As the blade passed, he felt pain in his nose.

Billy saw a flash. A shoe fell. Blood flowed. The knife dropped.

The guy dove for the blade. Billy stomped. He crushed the guy's hand. The guy jerked. Billy reached down. A black silk sock smashed Billy's face. Billy's tooth fell into the nose-blood pooling on the ground.

Billy leaned close and got hold of the knife's handle. He jabbed. There was resistance, then it was smooth.

There was blood on Billy's hand, shock on the guy's face. The smell of urine.

Billy pulled the knife and ran.

He went to the angel, and she smiled.

He called Sarah.

"What?"

"I just made a mistake."

"I don't give a shit about your fuck-ups Billy. I'm busy."

"Doing what?"

"Earning."

"I told you to stop. It's my job to take care of you."

"You don't fucking do it."

Billy heard a man's voice. Sarah hung up.

Billy sat at the base of the Angel and tied off. The needle was cold. He only had a bit of the Fentanyl left, he always kept one hit in reserve.

He threw the knife on top of the Angel. He took a step back, he couldn't see his blade. It blended well.

Tranquility edged in.

THE
HUSTLE

LIAM WAS MORALLY flexible, but only in the most rigid of ways. It helped when he worked a mark.

Tonight's bar, The Black Cat, floated like a Raymond Chandler fever-dream and the world was piss-yellow.

"Buy you a drink?"

The guy wasn't handsome... but his wedding-ring-tan was prominent. The Rolex looked cherry and ripe and ready.

JFK yammered on the tube and the cheap motel room felt moist.

The cheater snored. Liam wrote a note.

"Morty,
You tell the cops—I tell your wife.
Kisses,
Liam"

The pawn shop's manager said the Rolex was fake. Liam glided to the next adventure.

MAYBE I DON'T WANT TO BE FOUND?

BY WALDO OF "WHERE'S WALDO"

THE PRESENT CULTURE wars are focused on the merits of canceling. I am a simple man, and I am not fully equipped to wade into the stormy sea of this discussion. However, I pray we can all agree that stalkers are evil. With that in mind, perhaps cancel-culture could be wielded in a positive way? Can we, as a civilized society, agree to eliminate cancerous individuals from our lives? Do you, dear reader, realize the incessant hell that is spending your existence under a microscope? Allow me to enlighten you.

My torment started in England, in 1985. I noticed a man following me, taking my picture. I went to the bobbies to complain, but the stalking laws were weak, and this photog had not threatened me. I did my best to ignore the man. Eventually, I stopped noticing the intruder, and I assumed it was over. I was wrong.

In 1987, I saw the first book with my image on the cover: "Where's Wally?" My mind buzzed with confusion, and I felt sick. I bought the volume, went home, and read it cover to cover. I spent the next three weeks crying. Photos of me, at my most intimate, turned into a puzzle for some simple mind's amusement. My fashion sense became an "inside joke" for the masses.

We all desire to be part of something. I often seek out crowds to deal with my crushing loneliness and social anxiety. A man, an evil man, decided to exploit this. He made a game, a book, and a living, from exposing me. Disgusting. My personal existence, the very soul of my being, exploited for cheap consumer entertainment.

Throughout the late 1980s, I filed restraining orders and harassment lawsuits, to no avail. Eventually, I had enough, and was ready for a big change. I escaped to America in pursuit of the proverbial dream. The sun, the sand, the fast living, these were fun for a spell. After a time, I made my home in the more subdued city of Milwaukee and pursued my dream of being a cheese-critic.

Things were great, at first. My simple life progressed, and things began to look up. I had numerous articles published, "Monster Munster" being a high point. All were written under pseudonyms to ensure my stalker couldn't find me. I made friends and met a nice young woman. I changed my name from Wally to the more refined *Waldo*, hoping to ensure peace.

However, my tormentor returned.

"Where's Wally" became "Where's Waldo" and exploded in my adopted homeland.

Martin Handford is the beast's name. For 35 years, Handford has tortured my soul. Pursuing me, photographing me, exploiting me. Numerous cities, countries, and continents. Even a name change. Still, Handford haunts me.

In the spring of 2014, I was at the Museo del Prado in Madrid, enjoying contemplative stillness and fragrant coffee. It was quiet. I marveled at Diego Velázquez's "Las Meninas". Peace washed over me. I was content.

Eventually, I felt something amiss. I turned. Handford was in the gallery's corner. He ogled me, hands on hips. He displayed an erection. Metallica's *Master of Puppets* played from a tinny phone speaker in his pocket.

Handford smirked and asked, "Have you read Richard Connell?"

Being a man of refinement, I've taken in *The Most Dangerous Game*, Connell's seminal work, but I knew better than to engage my demon. I turned from the bastard Handford and ran to find security.

Handford bellowed: "The world is made up of two classes - the hunters and the huntees. I know which one I am, Waldo, and I know which one you remain." He cackled.

I dove into the arms of a dark-haired security guard. The man soothed me, and I wept.

I have not recovered. I've spent the last six years living as a hermit, hiding, destroyed.

I beg you: stop supporting Handford. Stop buying his disgusting, exploitive, books of invasive photos. These tomes are voyeuristic lifestyle pornography, focused on me. They are destroying my soul. Despite your personal position on cancel culture, Handford must be de-platformed.

Cancel Handford.

Where's Waldo? That is not for you to determine.

Maybe I don't want to be found?

A RED FLASH

CATCHING A BULLET was a possibility, but he was old and comfortable with dying. He waited for the sting.

Smitty was tired of moving so he sat on a mossy pile of bricks and sucked air through flared nostrils. It smelled like rotting vegetation.

He flexed his bad knee, the result of a bullet in Kosovo. His best friend died that day. No one remembered the U.S. fought in Kosovo. He was happy for the Iraq vets, they always got a thank you.

The sun was coming up over the Savannah River, everything was silent, and the world was calm.

Smitty was in the jungle that used to be Mulberry Grove Plantation. His Wal-Mart-Special tan slacks and pale-yellow dress shirt were no match for the briars. Sweat made polyester cling to skin.

He'd looked for the fugitive all night. If he could just find the little gangbanger he could get to bed. He had to get the job done. Duty mattered.

The bricks were hurting his ass. He was still out of breath when he stood.

Everyone thought he was in shape because he was thin. They were wrong. His ex-spouse was the cook. Ever since they split Smitty didn't eat enough. The thirty years of unfiltered Lucky Strikes probably didn't help.

Daylight broke. This was Smitty's first time at Mulberry Grove. Around here everyone was familiar with the historical marker. The place was home to Eli Whitney's invention of the cotton gin but going out to the actual sight… he didn't know anyone that bothered.

Old shit was all over Savannah, but no one paid attention. They were too busy with their own stuff. Smitty wondered if people still use the old cotton gins? Sometimes the old ways were best.

He began walking to his beat-up Ford Crown Victoria.

The sand fleas got in his mouth. They were chewy. Some voodoo lady from Pin-Point had a bug cure. The guys swore it worked, but he didn't take up with that trash.

He moved past a dead animal, it looked like a mule. It smelled strongly and he covered his nose.

He rounded the last bend and the modern world returned. His knock-off Rolex said it was almost time for lunch.

He got in the Crown Vic and headed to the meet up spot. Minutes later he pulled into the parking lot.

A group of officers stood idle in the humid air talking about a funeral for a motorcycle cop, heart attack.

Smitty got out and lit a Lucky Strike. He rubbed fatigue out of his light eyes and shook leaves out of cropped grey hair.

Smitty found Deputy Chief Flynn, "Want a cigarette, Boss-Man?"

Flynn never seemed to like Smitty. Smitty wasn't sure if it was because of his attitude, or his lifestyle.

"Those things'll kill you," Flynn said as he smiled and pulled out his cell-phone.

Everyone was buzzing about last night. It was the first car-chase for a lot of the new guys.

A voice came across the radio. "What's the fugitive's alias and what were his priors?"

Flynn pulled up his cellphone. Smitty reached for a piece of paper.

"Goes by Sonic," Flynn said.

"Like the fast food place?"

"Like the hedgehog."

The radio continued. "Priors are aggravated assault, domestic violence, moonshining, counterfeiting, and an accusation of homicide."

Smitty nodded at Flynn and went to the Crown Vic. "I'm going to do a drive by of the girlfriends. Find the hole, find the pole."

Flynn started calling after him, but Smitty had already closed the car door.

Driving always calmed him. He enjoyed the way the car handled. The thread-bare seats seemed molded to his ass. The motor pool officer wanted to get rid of it. It was the only one left in service.

He pulled over next to Yamacraw Village on the northwest side of Savannah. There was graffiti on the walls and trash on the ground. The girlfriend lived there with her aunt.

The residents of Yamacraw know a police car when they see one, but his was so old and beat-up they must have assumed it was an out-of-service auction buy. The car had a dark tint job. No one saw the old man inside.

He watched a couple hand to hand drug buys in the yard. How many foot chases and rough arrests had he done here… too many to count.

Smitty realized he'd probably locked up some of these kids' grandfathers. No one cared.

While watching the deals go down his phone rang. It was his ex.

"My half of the home sale equity check didn't come through… You ok Jim?"

Smitty smiled to himself. His ex still looked after him.

"I'll send it out today."

"Thanks."

"I'm doing ok. I'll drop my retirement paperwork in the spring."

"That's good. You deserve a break, do some fishing."

"I'd die from boredom."

"I got to go. If you need anything please reach out."

"Ok."

Things could've gone better with Eric. If he'd been home earlier and left the job at the office… maybe they would still be together.

Eric's new guy, Phil the pharmacist, seemed solid. His record was clean. But damn Phil was boring.

A young man that looked like the fugitive strolled past. Smitty thought about jumping out, old school style, but decided to follow policy, safety first and all that. Reaching for the radio he contacted Flynn.

"Call me on the cell," Flynn said.

Smitty punched up Flynn's number.

"I see the suspect."

"Got it. Hold tight."

Smitty received a group text message.

There was a picture of the bandit, a bio sheet, arrest record, a warrant, and the suspect's location.

Smitty radioed, "I'm staying here. Keeping eyes on."

Flynn texted. "Let's keep off the radio unless it is hot. Keep police business secure as possible. Reporters have frequency scanners."

The asshole actually signed his text *Deputy Chief Flynn*.

Smitty watched as the suspect moved towards an old

purple Cadillac. The car was more rust than metal. The rims were wire spoke, chrome, and immaculate.

He waited for a drug deal, but it never happened. The target was getting in the car. If the suspect hit the road he was gone.

Smitty responded to the group text. "We've got movement, how far out is the team?"

"15 minutes."

"Moving in to make contact."

"Hold off and wait for back-up."

"Negative. Time's up."

The Crown Vic humped the curb and groaned across the grass.

Smitty turned on the red and blues and opened the door. He took a kneeling position behind the engine block and drew his pistol. The adrenaline helped with the pain in his knees. He loved the rush, looked forward to it every time. He grabbed the megaphone.

"Put your hands on the headliner of the vehicle. No sudden movements."

The men in the vehicle raised their arms and stared at him, hard.

"Driver, with your left hand remove the car keys and place them on the roof. Open the trunk."

Smitty noticed people streaming from buildings.

Cellphones came out. Someone yelled "Worldstar!" Another yelled, "Fuck the police!"

Smitty continued. "Driver, with your left hand reach out the window and open your door."

The driver did as instructed.

"Step out of the car. Walk to the front. Keep your hands up and turn away from me."

The driver moved.

"Take your shirt off. If you have any weapons tell me."

"Ain't got shit."

"Walk backwards towards me."

When the man was fifteen feet from the car Smitty continued.

"Get on your knees and interlace your fingers behind your head."

The driver kneeled. Smitty moved. Three feet from the driver he holstered his weapon and started to pull his cuffs.

The gunshot was deafening.

Smitty's hearing distorted, like he had cotton in the lobes. Everything in his direct line of sight got brighter and sharper. The edges of his vision blurred. He kicked the kneeling man away.

The next volley of incoming shots sounded muffled.

Smitty dove to his right and drew his .40 caliber Glock 22.

There was a large oak to the front. He shot at the car and sprinted to the tree, diving into a pile of yellow fast food wrappers.

Smitty peeked around the trunk. Two shots flew past his head. He fired back until his Glock was empty and the slide locked back.

"Taking fire, get here right-fucking-now," he said on the radio.

A shot hit the bark. A bullet splashed into the dirt.

He slapped in his one spare fifteen round magazine.

He looked around and saw the top of the shooter's head, over the car's hood.

He focused hard on the front sight, aimed it at the hairline, and controlled his breathing.

Smitty squeezed.

The round fired. The weapon jumped. It caught him by surprise.

Time slowed. He felt recoil. The front sight rose and fell. The suspect's head snapped back. A flash of red mist.

Smitty moved right. The bandit was in the dirt. The back of the skull was gone, and a red pool was forming.

He put on cuffs. There was a pistol next to the body. Smitty removed the magazine.

He noticed it hurt to breathe. It was wet on his right side.

A woman fifty yards in front screamed, "He leakin!"

Sirens filled his ears, and everything went black.

Smitty saw a bright white light and hoped he was dead. He heard soft crying. It was Eric.

Smitty wondered if he brought Phil the Pharmacist?

"How you doing, babe?"

"Why do you treat yourself like this?"

"What happened?"

"He almost killed you."

"But I got him first."

"No one cared about that criminal. You need to keep yourself safe."

A smile crossed his face and the morphine hit his system.

Eric held his hand.

THE THUNDERBIRD MOTEL

ADRIANA DROVE HANK'S truck to Grove Bluffs Plantation and left her motorcycle at the strip club. Hank rode in the passenger seat. He was too beat-up to safely drive.

Hank won the fight. The drug dealer came in a close second.

Blood was messing up the truck's interior. The smell brought his mind back to the war and he didn't feel like dealing with that right now.

"So," Hank said. "Are we partners now?"

Adriana kept her eyes on the road.

"Yes, but it's a temporary thing," Adriana said. "I need a strong story to save my job. You need to figure out who really killed Kazinski."

"In it for number one?"

"Aren't we all?"

"You're quite the mercenary."

"Don't be so idealistic. We both want to get ahead. You need your brother out from under the Kazinski murder. For the time being our interests align."

"Got it."

"So Kazinski and that strip-club-pimping drug dealer were in it together?"

"Appears so."

"We got some good info out of him."

"Now we just have to avoid our favorite pimp's buddies."

"So, someone is after us?"

"Aren't they always?"

Adriana parked in front of the rotting plantation and helped him get out.

"It's spooky here. Sometimes I hate Savannah," Adriana said.

"What do you mean?"

"Your plantation freaks me out."

"Why?"

"How many slaves died building this?"

"Didn't think of that."

"I did."

Hank tried to put the key in the lock but was shaking too violently.

Adriana took over. She assisted him upstairs. Hank undressed. Adriana drew a hot bath. She left and Hank slid in.

"All right," Hank said to the open door. "Don't try to peek at my naughty bits. Pull up a seat. Let's talk this out."

"I'll try to contain myself."

Hank heard the wheels squeak on his office chair. He looked around the curtain. Adriana wore one of his old *Fight Night* T-shirts, a memento from his third mixed-martial-arts bout. Those skills seemed to have disintegrated.

"You found my dresser," Hank said.

"I'm an investigative reporter."

"So?"

"I investigated."

"That's fair."

"What are these crossed iron nails by the doors?"

"Voodoo crap from the last owner."

"You believe in that stuff?"

"No."

"Why don't you take them down?"

"I don't believe in Santa. I still like Christmas."

"You're different."

"I've heard that. How's your nose?"

"It stopped bleeding. The ankle hurts."

"Stilettos aren't the best footwear for fighting... but you were fashionable as hell."

"Funny. What about you? You look like hot garbage."

"Bath-water's the color of marinara sauce. The bleeding's stopped."

"I think you should go to the hospital."

"I'll survive."

"You sure?"

Hank knew he needed to open up if they were going to work this as true partners. He had to earn her trust. The borderline kidnapping they just performed pushed him towards honesty. The pimp gave them great info. They were going to prove his brother innocent. He could feel it.

Adriana was in deep and hadn't wavered.

"Since we're getting close and all," Hank said. "Did you hear about the recent shooting over at the Thunderbird Motel?"

"I did."

"What do you make of it?"

"It sounded like some gangland prostitute turf beef."

"You know of the victim, being a reporter and all?"

"I did..."

"On a scale of one to ten, how big of a piece of garbage is he?"

"Slappy? He sold heroin at playgrounds. I've lost friends to opiates. I would rate Slappy a ten. Why?"

"How do you feel about him getting shot?"

"Personally? He had it coming."

"Hardcore."

"I'm an Old Testament kind of girl."

"I'm the one that shot Slappy."

Adriana closed her eyes and breathed deeply. Hank was terrified that she would run out the door and call everyone. She turned to him.

"Why?"

"It shook out that way."

"Walk me through it."

"I learned Kazinski liked working girls, same reason we ended up at the club. I went to Thunderbird to ask around. Slappy turned up… one thing led to another."

"And?"

"He started shooting at me."

"So, it was self-defense?"

"Yes."

"But you shot him four times."

"I had to make sure he stayed down."

"Good."

"That's it?"

"Slappy'll be out of business for a while. One less overdose."

Hank looked at her and smiled.

"I think it's time to get out of the water," Hank said. "Can you give me a towel?"

Adriana handed it over and left the room.

Hank stepped out of the bath. He felt clean.

He walked downstairs. Adriana was making coffee. He noticed her laptop was open and there was a Word-Processor Document on the screen. was open and there was a Word-Processor Document on the screen.

"You getting a head start on the Kazinski piece?"

"Not exactly…"

The coffee pot was full when the police arrived. They read him his Miranda warning and he kept his mouth shut.

Hank was in the lock-up's common area when he saw the newspaper two days later.

Adriana's story on the Slappy shooting dominated the front page. She got a great article out of it. Hank was sure her career saw a boost. She stopped working the Kazinski murder when she took a promotion to Atlanta.

Slappy had a lot of friends in lockup. They saw the article as well.

THE
LAKE

ELI FELT THE stress-tick bouncing his left eye. His chest was on fire. It was a heart attack. The burden from his brother's lifetime of bad choices, his girlfriend threatening to leave, and his career burning to the ground finally became too much. This was the end, all of it was over, finally he could rest.

Then Eli remembered the pizza dinner. Pressure and tomato sauce were simulating the real thing.

"Passed out on the bathroom floor?" he asked.

"Pretty self-explanatory, your junkie brother is doped up again," Christy responded.

"Is he breathing? Do you have that opiate neutralizer, Narcan?"

"I don't know about Narcan. I don't know about drugs. You come home and deal with this. I'm going to work. I didn't sign up to babysit a 40-year-old."

"Christy, wait, I have that merger on Monday. I need to knock out the paperwork."

"I don't care about your merger. He's your twin. You deal with it."

"Babe, just give me a minute here."

"I'm leaving, you're lucky it's not for good."

"I know babe, just this one last time."

"Screw that, it's always one last time. I'm starting to think we want different things in life."

"I can fix the situ-"

"Stop. This is ridiculous."

Eli felt the guilt building inside, he knew she was reaching her limit, but what else could he do?

"Babe, I swear, I'm going to fix it. I'll cut him off, I'm done enabling."

Eli heard a door slam as the line went dead. Looking around he saw Jim, the regional manager, silhouetted against the plate glass window. It was overcast and drizzling outside, but the view of Atlanta's skyline from the 24th floor was still impressive.

Eli knew it was time for a solution. He internally debated doing something drastic for months, but the moment never felt right. Christy was on the verge of leaving him. Arnold was on the verge of dying. Eli's work was slipping, and people were noticing.

He sat sucking the sterile lemon scented office-air and dreading his choices. All of the options were shit.

Life without Christy seemed unbearable. She was the best thing in his world. Arnold wanted to get clean, but multiple stints in rehab proved that was unlikely.

"Hey Jim," Eli called across the cubicle farm. "Need to get home. A dang pipe burst in my bathroom."

"There sure are a lot of problems with your house lately! No worries, Christy like that hairdresser my wife recommended?"

"She did, said it's the best dye job ever, and you know I love the blondes! Plus, that seaweed body wrap got her down 10 pounds. She's happy as can be."

"That's great. Tell her the wife and I said hello, and I hope it all works out with your problem."

"Will do."

"By the way when are you and Christy getting married?"

"You sound like my mom," Eli said forcing a laugh through a plastic smile. "What's the rush? Why mess up a good thing? Change is painful!"

"Ha! I heard that. I've been meaning to ask, how's your brother?"

Jim just wouldn't let him go. "Getting better, slowly but surely. Also, I wanted to say thanks for understanding the situation last week. I was a little worried after the incident."

"Eli, you're a huge asset to this company. I like to think we are family here. Just because your brother made some bad choices, that doesn't change my opinion of you. However, going forward, security won't be letting him upstairs."

Eli felt the heat rising in his chest, Jim just wouldn't drop it, "Totally understand. I'm just glad the police didn't get called, and that all the blood came out of the carpet. I really owe you one."

"Like I said, no worries. Nothing steam-cleaning and a carpenter can't fix. See you Monday."

The relief washed over him as he finally escaped the office. Eli got in the elevator and exited on the first floor. He walked across the parking lot, past Jim's freshly waxed black BMW 7 series, to his beat-up silver 1996 Kia. He hopped in and started the drive home.

He took a left on Buford Highway and continued to Brookhaven. Absent-mindedly he looked at the meticulous landscaping, perfectly maintained homes, and botoxed housewives walking small dogs. It all reminded him that his life was a mess. They were identical twins, shared the same DNA, but ended up so different.

Ever since Arnold's back injury, the opiates were in control. First it was Percocet, but after a while the doctor stopped signing the prescriptions. That resulted in buying pills from friends. One thing led to another, soon he was mainlining heroin, free-will gone.

Eli took a left onto Dresden and turned into the townhouse's garage. He walked up the stairs to the second floor looking for Arnold.

He was lying on the chocolate carpet of the upstairs guestbedroom. An empty syringe lodged in his left arm, a tan braided leather belt was wrapped around the bicep. He was snoring loudly. Well, Eli thought, if you're snoring, you're breathing.

Looking down Eli couldn't believe how pale Arnold was. They'd always been fair-skinned, but lately Arnold looked like a sheet of paper. His blondish-brown hair was greasy and pushed back, his blue eyes were half-closed with large grey circles under each. His 6'1" 150 lbs. frame was all hard angles and sharp edges. Arnold looked like death.

Eli felt sick to his stomach. Damn it, he thought, why the hell is Arnold doing this to himself? How much money has the family spent on rehab? It was near $75'000 from Eli's own 401k. How could he fix this? How much more would Christy deal with? At what point do you stop throwing good money after bad? Eli pushed the thoughts from his mind.

This is your brother, your twin. Whatever it takes Eli must get it done, whatever it takes. If only Arnold could get off that junk. If only the dealers would leave him alone, then Arnold would have a chance. The dealers were the real problem.

Eli walked to the den, settled into the black leather couch, turned on a cheesy action movie, and tried to relax. As he watched Charles Bronson kill criminals in *Death Wish* he fell asleep.

An hour later Eli woke and checked on Arnold. His twin was still in the same spot, snoring loudly, talking in his sleep about a dead-mule and something called a haint porch on Weems plantation, gibberish.

He called Christy, she didn't answer, so he left a voicemail.

"Babe I promise I'll figure this out. You mean everything. I will not mess up our life together. I will fix it. I love you."

The thought of Arnold dying and Christy leaving was making him sweat. Loyalty was pulling his heart in two different directions. Eli grabbed a Bud Light and tried to unwind.

Looking back, it all seemed surreal. Arnold was the good one. The natural athlete. His talent and hard work led to a scholarship to play college baseball.

Eli wasn't as athletic, so he went to school on an Army scholarship. After 5 years in the Army, 3 of it in the 75th Ranger Regiment, he went into private military contracting. A few years of getting shot at for big money swelled his bank account before he moved back home.

The military paid for his Master's in business from the University of Georgia, and that landed him the good banking job. But Uncle Sam extracted his pound of flesh, nothing came for free. 24 months in Iraq was a steep price to pay. The nightmares and survivor's guilt were a bitch, but that's how it goes.

Sometimes he missed being back in-country. Problems were simple there and a bullet took care of most. However, he reminded himself, stuff like that would get you arrested in the states.

"Wake up, asshole. Christy is about to leave me and you're about to kill yourself," Eli said as he lightly kicked his brother's ribs. Arnold didn't respond.

All that war and he came home to this. He wished he could handle Arnold's pusher like the bomb makers of Baghdad. No matter what the bleeding-heart liberals said, violence got shit done.

Opiates and the vultures that sell them, both doctors and dealers, ruined Arnold's life. Now the blowback was ruining Eli's. He knew a choice must be made. He should cut Arnold off, but he just couldn't. There was another way to solve the problem, he just needed to find it.

Eli's phone rang.

"He still on our floor?" Christy asked.

"Yea, hasn't moved, but he's breathing," Eli said.

"You have to get a handle on this. I did not sign up to play nursemaid. We're supposed to be married, have a house, and be working on having a kid by now."

"We can still practice making kids."

"It's not the time to joke."

"I know babe, I'll figure something out."

"I already figured it out. You need to cut him off. I want more out of life."

"I want more too babe. I want you happy, and I want Arnold healthy. Don't worry, I'll solve it. If that dealer would leave him alone all this would be over. Every rehab stint he does great, until that scum-bag Carl comes around."

"Whenever I bring this up you talk about the last rehab stint. I don't care. This is Arnold's fault, no one else. I love you babe, and I love him. But I'm at the end of my rope," Christy said as she hung up.

Eli looked down at his snoring brother.

"I'm going to Panera to get some food, bye."

Arnold didn't move.

He walked home eating his sandwich and thought about the dealer, Carl. That sketchy little scumbag went to high school with them, St. Pius, in Atlanta. He was the only drug-dealer there. A lot of the kids' families were wealthy. Carl made a killing It was almost 20 years later, and he was still pushing the same crap to the same kids, at least the ones that hadn't overdosed. Eli could think of at least 5 lives Carl personally destroyed.

Fuck Carl, Eli thought, he is only 5'6 and out of shape… I could kick his ass. But what would that accomplish? Carl would probably call the cops and get Eli arrested, who would help Arnold then? If only he could put a round right between those beady little brown eyes. It was so much simpler in Iraq. Back in the war violence solved everything. He started to understand his choice.

As he got back home, he saw that Arnold moved from the floor to the bed.

"You awake?"

There was no response.

"Christy is about to leave me, and my boss is losing his patience. You're killing us. I lose my job and we are both homeless."

Arnold's phone started vibrating, it was Carl. The text was a single question mark. Something shifted in Eli's mind. He realized what had to be done. He'd known the answer for months, but never admitted it to himself. Something finally changed.

He needed to kill Carl.

Carl vanishing would solve it all. There would be room to breathe, room to heal.

He needed to kill Carl.

The idea terrified him, but he felt relief. The end was in sight. His heart rate spiked and beads of sweat rolled down his forehead. It would all be over soon, cut out the cancer and the body can live.

Eli's stomach turned as he developed a plan in his head. He knew that if he covered his face, bought stuff with cash, did his research at a public library, and didn't use his car he would be hard to track. But, with the consequences so dire he must be perfect. Logically he was fine with killing Carl, even welcomed it. But his mind kept flashing back to the consequences. This wasn't a warzone, if he got caught, he was ruining three lives. Perfection was the only option. He could not let down Christy. He could not fail Arnold.

Eli rode his bicycle to the library across town. Arriving and looking around he did not see any security cameras. He put on a hat and sunglasses before going inside.

He sat at an open computer. He searched for deep lakes in rural areas. There was a bridge that went over Lake Chatuge in a remote port of western North Carolina, near the Georgia border, about two hours north of Atlanta. The isolated location meant minimal police coverage. His resolve deepened, it was worth the risk. The cancer had to go.

He went to the other side of the library and found a road almanac. He looked it over and memorized the route to the bridge.

Leaving the library, he rode to a drug store. Still wearing the hat and sunglasses he bought a set of dishwashing gloves, a couple bottles of bleach, three rolls of paper towels, and a hair net. He used cash.

Next, he rode to Home Depot and bought a set of painter's coveralls, a large painter's drop cloth, and duct tape.

He shoved all the supplies in his backpack and went home.

The pressure was building. He couldn't drive the thoughts of disappointing Christy or failing Arnold from his head. He wondered if he should wait, put it all off until he had time to really dig into the plan. He drove it from his mind, a good plan now is better than a perfect plan too late.

Inside his house, he placed the hat, sunglasses, clothing, and backpack into a large trash bag. He soaked all the contents in bleach and threw in some tomato sauce for good measure.

Then he rode to the taco place down the street, Verde, and put it all in the dumpster.

Back home he picked up Arnold's cell phone. There were only three numbers saved, Eli's, Carl's, and Papa John's, the pizza joint. Scrolling through the texts he came to the last correspondence from Carl and sent a text message.

I got $20, can you come over? Eli typed.

The response was immediate.

Fuck you, always lying with your bitch ass. You nothin but a punk bitch junkie.

Eli sent a photo of the money.

Aight, on my way dog. You playin me you WILL be sorry. I'm always strapped wit one in the chamber play-boy!

Eli placed the drop cloth on the floor near the entrance. He picked up Arnold's wooden Louisville Slugger baseball bat, still dinged up from the glory days. Eli knew that Arnold gave Carl a key to the townhouse. He got into the coat closet near the front door, sucked in the aroma of moth balls, and waited.

30 excruciating minutes later he heard the front door open. Adrenaline dumped into Arnold's body. His vision started to tunnel, and his mouth became dry. He had never killed a man outside of the war. If he was caught, he would probably get the death penalty, Christy's face would be all over the news, and Arnold would surely overdose.

He reminded himself that this was righteous, this was justice, and this was the only way. He was getting rid of filth and saving his brother. The plan was good, he wouldn't get caught. He gripped the bat harder to combat the sweat coming from his palms.

"Yo, Arnold, where you at son?" Carl called out.

Carl was from a white upper-middle-class suburban home. His dad was an accountant, and his mom was a nurse. The fact that he tried to talk "Ghetto" was just another thing that pissed Eli off.

Silently, Eli stepped out from the coat closet. Heart pounding out of his chest. He raised the bat over his head and brought it down like an axe. It landed clean. There was a loud *THUMP*, a crisp *POP*, and the dealer dropped. Carl was breathing but wasn't moving. There was no blood.

Putting on the dishwashing gloves, coveralls, and hair net, Eli stripped Carl naked. He put Carl's clothes in a grocery bag. Then he took the battery from the cellphone and put it in his pocket.

Using duct tape Eli covered Carl's mouth, bound his hands behind the back, and wrapped his legs together from the ankles to the knees. He wrapped Carl in the drop cloth and then secured the whole mess with tape. Eli stuffed the package into a wheeled black Samsonite bag.

Eli rolled it to the stairs and muscled it to the garage. He loaded the bag into the back of his Kia.

He grabbed Carl's car keys and hit the lock button. Eli heard the horn beep, identified Carl's white 2016 Audi A7 and made a mental note to move it when he got back. Next, he started his drive to the bridge.

After an hour he heard thumping and shouts from the trunk.

"Be quiet or I will put a bullet in your head," Eli yelled. The noise stopped.

Eli pulled out his phone and called Christy.

"Hey babe, I am going out to get a bite to eat. What time will you be home?"

"I'm staying at my mom's for a while. I don't know how much more of this crap I can take. I want us to be together. I need to be your focus."

Carl coughed in the back.

"What was that?" Christy asked.

"Nothing, you're my focus babe. It's all about to get better, I promise." Arnold hung up.

They arrived in the Appalachian town of Hiawassee at about 6:30 p.m., it was a Tuesday. Eli thought about the timing and decided to wait for the deep night. Absent-mindedly he realized the area was beautiful, full of gently rolling mountains and deep green vegetation.

At 1:30 a.m., he sensed the time was right. He drove over the bridge and parked in the middle of the span. Stepping out into the clear night air he popped the trunk. This would solve the problem. Besides, he'd done a lot worse for a lot less.

Grasping both ends of the bag he lifted the 160lb package and threw it over the side. Carl's cell phone and battery went next. He supposed he could have killed Carl first, or dosed him with heroin, but he wanted the dealer to suffer.

Quickly he drove away. The drop took less than 30 seconds. Carl was already at the bottom of a lake, and it was over.

He got home around 3 a.m. Immediately he got into Carl's A7. Eli drove to the middle of a rough area of town near Buford Highway. Using the bleach and paper towels, he wiped down the inside of the car. He put the keys in the ignition, rolled down the windows, and rode away. As he passed a corner, he threw the cleaning supplies in a trash can near a bus stop. The residents would have the Audi gone in seconds.

When Eli got home, he cleaned his Kia's trunk. He put all the night's clothing and various supplies into two black trash bags. He poured bleach into the trash bag and soaked the contents. Then he went to the dumpster behind Sushi Yoshino on Johnson Ferry Road, and shoved the bag in. The stench of rotting seafood was over-powering.

Eli stepped into the shower at 5 a.m. He knew that he'd done right by his brother. Eli was sure Arnold could get clean this time. The dealer was gone. He cut the problem off at the source.

Waves of relief flowed over him. He couldn't wait to call Christy, tell her it would all be ok.

The killing was for a good purpose. Besides, it was a one-time thing. Eli knew that violence, used righteously, fixed problems.

As he got out of the shower Eli heard Arnold's phone start vibrating. Eli looked at the text, it was from Papa John's. He thought about ignoring it, but then asked himself why in the hell a pizza place would be texting anyone.

Hey, I got some new stuff in. You got cash?

THE MISSIONARY

JIMMY HATED FEELING the delicate orbital bones splinter, but he didn't have a choice. He needed to be free. It was unfortunate.

He detested beating on the missionary, watching the eyes go chalky. But he knew any good man was willing to kill for his family. If he got out, he could send money to Sarah. Family... that's what all this was all about.

Jimmy pulled the body into the thick brush beside Highway 17. He stripped the corpse and changed. The clothes fit well, except the shoes. He kept on his jail-issued sneakers.

He looked down at the black polyester slacks, short-sleeve button-down shirt, red-patterned tie, and nametag, Elder O'Callaghan- The Church of Jesus Christ of Latter-day Saints. Jimmy grew up in Utah in the middle of the U.S.A. He knew the Mormon Missionary thing well.

He left O'Callaghan under a pile of leaves. He wasn't worried about being caught. The coyotes would clean up before it started to stink.

There were not many houses in the South Georgia countryside. After walking for an hour, he came to a small beige trailer. A woman sat on the front steps. She could be thirty or sixty.

She looked him up and down. Her eyes were eager. Jimmy's twenty pounds of jail muscle and sharp features meant conning middle-aged women, or men, was cake. He was always happy to trade a good time for what he needed.

The woman tamped out her cigarette. She wore no wedding ring.

"Hello sister," Jimmy said, "Have you heard the good news?"

He reached out, they shook hands. She held on too long.

"Jesus is my savior, you want to tell me more?"

"I'd love to, sister. I'm Elder Joe O'Callaghan."

"I'm Roberta Hansen-Ford."

"Can I come in and spread the word?"

She smiled and nodded.

"Give me one moment to straighten up, then you come in and I'll get you some lemonade."

Jimmy felt her eyes. They were hungry. She went inside. After fifteen minutes she said, "Door's open."

Jimmy strolled in. He saw plastic over a cheap plaid sofa. There was a pressboard table holding a King James Bible and a Book of Mormon. Military awards hung on the walls. In some places the paint was darker, some photos had been recently taken down.

"Getting ready to move," Jimmy said. "Do you need help?"

He hated taking advantage of a lonely woman, but he needed to support Sarah. This was how he did the right thing.

"So kind of you to ask, but no. I'm recently divorced. The pictures of my ex-husband were painful."

Jimmy realized this was going to be easy.

"I understand. I see you already have some of Joseph Smith's testament?" He stood close, letting her feel his presence.

"O yes, another missionary came by a few months back. He left the book but didn't have time to chat."

"Sometimes my brothers get overwhelmed spreading the news."

"That's unfortunate."

"I promise to take my time."

He talked about church for fifteen minutes, then started flirting, light touching. Roberta was eating it up. Soon she brought out wine. He played good Mormon boy. Roberta seemed to relish being the temptress. After two bottles she led him to the bedroom.

They made love.

Afterward, he ran to the bathroom and pulled up fake tears.

"I'm a horrible person," he said. He tried to sell it hard.

"No, you were bringing me comfort in a time of need. You're a good man," Roberta said as she massaged his shoulders. "You've done the right thing. What can I do to make you feel better?"

His chance.

"I'm so upset. I cannot believe what I've done. Can you just drive me home? This is all too much."

"Of course. Let me find the keys."

She walked out of the bedroom.

Jimmy heard rummaging in the next room. He looked for something heavy to knock her out, kill her quick. He didn't want anyone to suffer. He found a marble bust of Julius Caesar.

It felt like a truck hit him from behind.

A thousand hornets buzzed in his ears, stinging him in unison. As quick as the suffering came it was gone.

He heard Roberta, voice was different.

"Where did you get those clothes and why are you wearing prison shoes?"

Jimmy was confused. How did she know? What did she know?

"Roberta, wait. Prison shoes? What?"

The pain returned. He pissed a little. He couldn't think.

"Stop messing around. That was ten seconds. Next ride is twenty."

"Ma'am, you got it wrong, please…"

She started crying and the agony returned. The whole world was pain.

He looked up. Roberta held something boxy and black.

He saw a flash, his right eye stung. He heard Roberta sobbing.

"My maiden name is O'Callaghan."

There was a flash. Then the pain left.

THE EXIT

RODRIGO SLAPPED AWAY the incoming jab, down and to the left, shifting his weight. Juan countered with a straight right.

Rodrigo dropped his hips, ducking under the punch. He drove forward, planted his left ear in Juan's side, and hit a double leg takedown, exploding skyward.

He guided Juan down, driving his left shoulder in and through. All of his two hundred and twenty-five pounds focused on the younger man's gut.

OOMPH.

The impact with the blue mats was violent. Air shot out of Juan. He sounded like a balloon deflating.

"Asshole! Not so hard!" Juan screamed, flat on his back, driving his right knee into the open space, trying to move his hips in front of Rodrigo, get to guard.

Rodrigo pushed the knee, rotated right, passing. He was flat on top of Juan. He popped up, kneeling on Juan's stomach.

Rodrigo rained down elbows, too hard for practice. He wanted to smash the little prick.

Juan shifted left, then right, trying to off-balance Rodrigo. It didn't work. The third elbow snuck through. Rodrigo felt the satisfying dry-pasta snap of a broken nose.

"FUCK! Tap! Stop!" Juan said, flecks of blood fountaining up.

Rodrigo wanted to continue, but there was no honor in being a bully.

"Why you going so hard?" Juan pinched his nose and leaned his head back. His tan skin and black hair covered in sweat.

Rodrigo couldn't stand the bullshit games. Juan knew what was up, no reason to play dumb, but he would spell it out.

"You threw that fight. You made the gym look bad. Plus, you didn't tell me. I could have made the right bets. So, you embarrassed both of us and I didn't make any money," Rodrigo replied, spitting into the pooling blood on the mat. His Brazilian accent was thick, but he was trying hard to improve his English.

"I should have let you know."

"Clean up this mess," Rodrigo said, waving to the congealing liquid.

Juan ran to the backroom, grabbed bleach and paper towels, and started scrubbing. The cleaning products' smell mixed with the stale sweat. Rodrigo's head started to spin as he stood over the younger man.

Rodrigo wasn't tall, only 5'10', but he was solid. His steroid-fueled muscle and twenty years of training meant he put off a "don't fuck with me" vibe.

Juan didn't have that air about him. He looked like any other young Latino kid, covered in tattoos, dark hair bleached platinum. He was the same height as Rodrigo, but skinny.

"You little prick. I brought you here from Rio I gave you a life, this merda is how you repay me."

"Yea, you did it all out of the goodness of your heart. Don't forget you needed an investor for your gym, and you wanted my dad's money," Juan said, still cleaning.

It took every ounce of restraint Rodrigo had not to smash the smug little prick.

"We have a good thing. The steroids made us cash. The fake gym memberships made the money clean. The real gym memberships, and winning fights, earned us respect. We have the strongest jiu-jitsu team in Jacksonville. We own the building. We have money in the bank, no debt. We are about to stop selling. I came to the U.S., took a chance, and now I can get out clean. And your dumb ass wants to risk the cops looking at us for what? Making a few thousand bucks throwing a fight?"

"I made ten grand."

Rodrigo kicked him in the ribs, hard.

"PORRA! Stop!" Juan yelled.

"My friend, I have a wife and two kids. You know Flavia has all those medical problems. Why in the hell are you risking everything for ten thousand dollars?"

"I didn't think it through."

"No shit." Rodrigo sat down, started wiping the mats with Juan. "I'm sorry for the kick. I shouldn't lose my cool. But after tonight we are free. We pay off Jacare and it's over. We have a building, a business, a home, a life. We have nothing to worry about, forever."

"I know, I'm sorry tio."

"It's ok. Just stop doing stupid shit."

They finished cleaning. Juan went to the locker room and put on a fresh white jiu-jitsu kimono and black belt with a red tip. Rodrigo put on a Carioca Fighting Systems polo shirt and went to the front desk.

The bored soccer moms and soft suburban dads streamed in, dropping off spoiled kids. Rodrigo kissed all their asses, he was happy to. Anything was better than going back to that ghetto favela in Rio.

He came to the United States on a tourist visa with ten dollars and some fighting skills. He didn't even speak English. Fifteen years later he was a citizen with two daughters, a wife he loved, and a successful business. The U.F.C. thing hadn't worked out, but it got his name in the paper. Now he owned the biggest gym in North Florida.

Juan was Rodrigo's best friend's younger brother. He was a good fighter, but he liked to party and did things without thinking. Rodrigo loved the kid, but sometimes it was a challenge.

The children's class wrapped up at 4 p.m. After the lesson, Juan flirted with some of the moms.

"Stop trying to fuck those housewives. We don't want to piss off their husbands," Rodrigo said, laughing.

They showered and put on clean clothes, a red polo shirt and jeans for Rodrigo, blue board shorts and a white t-shirt for Juan. Rodrigo went to the safe and grabbed the duffel bag with the fifty grand, handing it to Juan.

"All right, we drop this with Pedro and we're out. We did it, my friend." Rodrigo put a hand on Juan's shoulder. Juan hugged him.

Then headed outside and got in Rodrigo's white BMW X1. They drove south to Orlando. It was hot, steamy, and mosquitoes were everywhere, but Rodrigo liked it. It reminded him of home.

The ride was boring, but the Samba music was good. Juan told lies about all the different American women he'd been with over the past two years. He claimed they couldn't resist his Latin charm. Rodrigo had heard all the stories multiple times and knew they were bullshit. The fighting had messed up Juan's face, his ears looked like chewed gum, but Rodrigo let it slide. Juan was just young and cocky, if he ever treated a woman half as good as he treated his bulldog, he would be a happy man. Plus, the kid had real talent. He could be a champion one day... if he kept working at it.

They pulled in front of Jacare's steakhouse, Fogo De Brasil, two and a half hours later. They went inside and nodded to Silvana, the dark-haired silicone-enhanced hostess, entering the back office. Pedro, Jacare's second in command, was sitting behind the desk.

"Playboy!" Pedro said, standing. "How are you, my friend? You want a caipirinha? A little cerveja? I have Corona."

"No, we're good. Just came to pay off Jacare," Rodrigo said, looking around the office. The decoration was blue-neon, stainless steel, and faux-crystal. It smelled like roasting meat.

Pedro raised his eyebrows, "You're serious about getting out?"

Rodrigo nodded and shook Pedro's hand, Juan hugged him. They sat down in two overstuffed black leather chairs facing the desk.

"We all thought you were joking," Pedro said.

"It's over. We own the gym," Rodrigo said, waving at Juan. "We own our condos. We have two hundred members on monthly contract. It is time to move on."

Pedro smiled. He pulled a drawer and presented three glasses plus a bottle of Johnny Walker Blue label.

"This calls for a toast. You did it the right way. Stopping while you're winning. We appreciate you setting us up with that new distribution channel," Pedro said, winking.

Rodrigo grabbed two drinks, passing one to Juan. Pedro reached over, they clinked glasses and swallowed.

They sat, smiling, enjoying each other's company. They talked about Rio and the old days for thirty minutes, switching between Portuguese and English. They told the old stories and laughed at the old jokes. Rodrigo promised to come back for Pedro's daughter's eleventh birthday party next month. Eventually, Rodrigo turned to Juan.

"Pass him the money, it's time to go."

Juan smiled and nodded. He turned to his right and reached down. When he came up, Rodrigo noticed the kid's face was different.

BOOM.

The sound of the first gunshot confused Rodrigo. He hadn't heard one since he left the City of God favela in Rio twenty years back.

A large red blotch formed on Pedro's white shirt, near the right nipple. Pedro looked down, surprised, silent. The second round hit him below the left eye. His head snapped back, a red mist coated the wall.

Rodrigo turned to Juan. He didn't feel surprised or angry, it was all happening faster than his emotions could react.

"I didn't say I wanted to retire." Juan smiled.

A hot bolt of lightning sliced through Rodrigo's gut. He fell over, not understanding.

Juan put the gun in Rodrigo's hand. Then he put it against his own shoulder. Juan gripped over Rodrigo's hand and made Rodrigo squeeze the trigger. The gun bucked and fell. A valley formed in the meat.

"PORRA! FUCK!"

Juan punched Rodrigo in the nose, hard. Rodrigo felt it break.

As Rodrigo faded, he heard Juan call Jacare, saying Rodrigo tried to rob Pedro, but he'd stopped it, and saved the day.

"Yes," Juan said. "The asshole's still alive, barely."

Juan played samba from his phone as Rodrigo floated away.

THE
MASK

HECK THOMAS WAS an empty husk. Every day bled into the next. Being a cop was an endless stream of chases and fights and screams and sadness.

He missed Iraq. Yes, it sucked. Yes, he dealt with survivor's guilt and shitty dreams. A lot of good men died, and a lot of funerals were attended. However, back in Iraq he had a purpose.

Now Heck existed in gray. He went through the motions and paid his taxes and lived in a fog.

Hunting Savannah's criminals was never ending and infinitely pointless. They kept coming. It was like trying to stop the tide.

Heck tried volunteering at the Special Olympics... hoping to find a purpose. It did nothing for him. He went to a church, but the hole wasn't filled. The reason never came.

He sat in his beat-up Ford Explorer and looked at the swaying live oaks with their Spanish moss. He sucked in the pollen and listened to the crickets. He steadied himself and opened the door. He shifted his mind to work.

"I have a new fugitive warrant," Heck said to the other cops gathered around the SUV's hood. "She's an illegal wanted for dealing crystal and jumping the border. She has a long rap sheet, to include attempted murder."

Heck passed around a series of pictures to the other officers on his team.

Someone called from the back of the formation, "What's her particulars?"

"Maria Hernandez," Heck said. "Mexican national, 5 foot 4, two hundred pounds, and it's not muscle. Brown hair and eyes."

"You just described yourself," Gill said.

"I'm taller than that, asshole," Heck said. "Maria has a tattoo of the grim-reaper on her left forearm. She lives with her tweaker boyfriend, a white guy named Teddy. Teddy has some minor warrants for possession. We're after Maria. We have a search warrant for the criminal only, so no digging through drawers. Fourth amendment is our guide, don't fuck that up. If we find the boyfriend but no Maria, we are going to tell him he has a choice: Go to jail or give her up."

"What's the order of entry?"

"Bobby's the breacher. Get that big ass upfront and take down the door," Heck said.

"I am a svelte two ninety and my butt looks great. At least that's what Gill's ex-wife tells me," Bobby said.

"The first ex or the second? Scratch that, doesn't matter," Gill said. "Do me a favor and marry one so I can stop paying alimony."

"Let's talk about work, not Gill's shit personal choices. It's time to go."

A line of dark cars drove to the target house. A hundred yards out they parked. The team approached on foot.

They pulled their .40 caliber Glock pistols and shouldered military-style M4 rifles.

Looking at the place made Heck sad. The home was a single

story with faded blue paint and broken windows. The front-porch was sagging, the lights were on. It smelled of mold and damp lumber.

A few random patrol officers took the back and sides. Heck, Gill, Bobby, and a patrolman moved to the porch. Gill was first. He was tall and skinny and old. He knocked three times.

"Police with a warrant," Heck said. "Open the door,"

The interior lights cut off.

"Breacher up!"

Bobby moved in and swung the ram. The particle board door splintered. The entrance exploded into the darkness of the house.

The scent of sweat and ammonia came out in a moist cloud. Bobby stepped back so Gill could get the bullet resistant shield in front of the team.

Heck's pulse jumped. "Smells like cat piss. That means meth." Heck's hands went clammy and the hair on the back of his neck stood up.

"Two cover right then move left," Heck said. "Forward as a unit. I'll hold the hallway."

They checked behind the damp couch and secured the living room.

"Stay alert, we know someone is home because of those lights," Heck said.

They moved into the first bedroom. A television rested against the wall. The set was an old tube model, covered in dust. A VCR sat nearby.

A threadbare corduroy recliner rested in front. There was a small metal table with a jar of Vaseline, a clear glass meth pipe, and a crusty white rag.

The television was playing a tape showing a man in a sleeveless AC/DC t-shirt, crotchless zebra print tights, and a mask from the movie *Scream*.

The man in the video was masturbating furiously. Based upon the position of the chair and the surrounding material someone had been pleasuring themselves to this video while smoking crystal meth.

Gill looked at Heck and winked. "He's jerkin it hard. Good technique."

"Let's move," Heck said. "This house is in the middle of the ghetto. The lights are not hooked up to a timer. Someone is in this house, we just haven't found them. Call in the K9."

The officer and his dog, Hero, pulled up to the house an hour later.

Hero started indicating that the master bed needed to be re-searched.

"Something's behind the headboard," Gill said.

Heck gave the thumbs up, the bed was pulled, and the team shifted forward.

Heck saw a phantom in the wall.

"Hands," Heck said, "Let me see your hands!"

The figure behind the headboard stuck two empty mitts out and jumped into the bedroom.

Bobby cuffed up the wall-dweller.

They backed out of the house with their prisoner. Using the K9 they re-cleared and secured the building.

The prisoner had the sunken prematurely aged face of a heavy drug user. Most of his teeth were rotted out and his skin was porcelain-white.

He wore a cut-off AC/DC shirt and basketball shorts with zebra print tights underneath.

The man was the performer in the video.

"Holy Shit," Gill said. "He was jerking it watching himself jerking it!"

"Wait…" Bobby said. "That surprises you? You assholes didn't know about the ole' masturbation infinity loop?"

A THERAPEUTIC DEATH

Heck turned and looked at him. "What's a masturbation infinity loop?"

"You make a video of yourself jerking it. Then you jerk it, watching the video of yourself jerking it. Then you jerk it, forever."

"Plus, smoke lots of meth."

"The meth is critical."

The prisoner was led over to a dark blue Ford Explorer. Heck told the team to wait by the porch. Heck went to talk to Teddy alone.

"I don't care about your little bullshit state warrants or a little bit of crystal," Heck said. "I am going to give you a choice. You give me Maria, or you go to jail. Please remember it's hard to get drugs in jail."

Heck watched Teddy's light blue eyes twitch. He was so thin and pale he seemed more spirit than man.

"All right," Teddy said. "Fuck that bitch."

"That's what I like to hear," Heck said. "Before we move on, can I trust you? Do I have your word?"

"Of course. I love the cops. I always wanted to join the force."

Heck tried not to laugh directly in Teddy's face.

"Fair enough," Heck said. "Where is she?"

"On the green-line bus," Teddy said. "She's on her way here."

"You have her number?"

"No, she doesn't like cell phones. Say's they're too easy to track."

Heck and Teddy talked a bit more but nothing else of value came out. They cut Teddy loose and got back on the road.

Heck and his team spent two hours pulling over every city bus they could find. They never saw Maria.

Heck called his boss but got forwarded to voicemail.

The team arrested seven more people that night. Heck felt dead inside.

On the drive home Heck thought about his mom back in Atlanta. He promised himself he would call her in the morning. He was going to request a transfer to be closer to her. He needed a change. He got home to his empty basement apartment and fell asleep alone.

CATCH

I SQUEEZE THE wheel and look over. Smitty's pupils are dilated.

"Turn that down." *Master of Puppets.* "That the guy?"

Smitty nods, he's scared. Me too, but no one knows. I got that Aurelius face. Also, I don't care if I die. That helps.

"He drivin'."

"Fuck that guy."

I check my seatbelt and mash the pedal to the floor. I hear a pop and see glass-snowflakes, the bandit dropped his gun. Smoke and steam rise from a crumpled blue hood and it smells sweet, antifreeze. James Hetfield roars.

"We got a runner!" I'm out and on top. I get the cuffs on, and curse words stream out. So many body cameras, zero force... other than the car thing. I'm gentle.

"Holy shit, that was cool."

"Normal day at the office." I'm so full of shit. I've never done that before, life isn't a movie. "I'm going to knock out paperwork. Can you talk to the reporters?"

I cry in my car, I miss my wife and I miss my daughter and I miss my dog and why the fuck did I trade them for a stupid fucking job that pays shit?

Smitty gives me a thumbs up. I smile and return it, wave him off.

I check my phone, there are no missed calls, no texts. I should have died in Baghdad. Maybe I did die in Baghdad. God, I wish I died in Baghdad.

Got a murderer today.

DEAD CAMEL

THE IMPROVISED EXPLOSIVE popped off to the convoy's left. The armored black Suburban Neil drove muffled the sound to a dull thud. The blast seemed smaller than normal.

"Anyone hurt?" the medic, Luiz, called across the radio.

The team members, in four matching Suburbans, all responded that they were good.

"Why is my windshield covered in rotten meat? Was that fucking bomb hidden in a dead camel?" the medic asked.

"Nope, it was a God-Dammed camel carcass," was the radioed response.

"We dismounting and checking it out?" Neil asked the team leader, Joe, who was seated in the front passenger's seat.

"Fuck that. Those small ones are bait. I'm not leaving my air-conditioning, we're not takin the bait," Joe responded in his thick Cajun accent.

The team was all ex-military; The team was all ex-military: seven Americans, four Brits, two Aussies, and a Kiwi. They transported aid workers, provided security for doctors, and trained non-profits in the basics of staying alive in Iraq.

"Where are we going again? Been running so hard I've lost track," Neil asked.

"East, cuttin across this bombed-out shithole on Qadisaya

towards Al-Zawra park. Got to give these pills to the do-gooders over at that pop-up clinic ran by Médecins Sans Frontières. We'll be home for dinner." Joe responded.

"Why the hell are we leaving so damn early? It's the ass-crack of dawn."

"None of these terrorists get up at 0600, we're out-smarten em. I'm one of this generation's great tactical minds!"

From the driver's seat Neil turned his green eyes to Joe. Neil had been with the unit for about a month. Joe was on his second year as commander. The two of them were still feeling each other out. Joe always rode in the passenger seat of Neil's truck.

"What ya think about that little bomb?" Neil asked.

"Like I said, bait. Luckily for the team, I'm a master-baiter. I think those assholes are trying to see how we react, draw us out, and attack. Fuck that and fuck them, keep driving," Joe responded.

"And fuck Baghdad," Neil said.

"And fuck Baghdad. But shit, it's more fun than some desk job. All I ever wanted was a gig that got my heart going and a faithful woman. Getting half of what you want is pretty good," Joe responded, laughing and spitting Copenhagen into an empty water bottle.

"Fuckin' A. I'd rather suck-start my pistol than work a desk job or get re-married. You said you were Marine Recon before, right?" Neil asked. After two months he figured he should know more about Joe.

"Damn straight, Semper Fi!" Joe said while flashing a toothy grin. Neil realized Joe must have come from money, his orthodontic work was too perfect, "Someone say you were SF?"

Neil thought back to his time in the Army's Special Forces. He had gone to war in Columbia, the Philippines, Bosnia, Nigeria, and all over the Middle-East.

"24 years. Uncle Sam took care of me."

"Well, that was thick. That how your arm got jacked up?"

Neil loved that about a war zone. No one had time to beat around the bush. They said what was on their mind, fuck your feelings.

"Moro firebomb in the Philippines. Most of my right side got hit. Third degree burns."

Looking down at the scar tissue on his forearm Neil thought back on all those years. In basic training, he had stood 6 feet tall. Now he was 5'10. His non-scarred skin was tan and leathery. The worry lines around his mouth were deep. A stray bullet had hit his right leg in Bosnia and gave him a slight limp. His hair turned grey a few years back. He still kept it short and had grown a matching beard.

"Married?"

"Divorced, she cheated on me after a while. Some women just don't deserve all this sexiness," Joe responded. His brown eyes radiated warmth. It made Neil realize how miserable he was, and how charming Joe was. He wanted what Joe had.

"They should issue divorce papers in basic. I'm lucky I only have one. Some of these boys are on number 4. That's an expensive hobby,"

"The kiwi has it figured out. He's got one of those open relationships. Maybe I need to get me a different woman. I can be very progressive. You got anyone back home?"

"Divorced. She was a good woman. But she needed a husband, and my daughter needed a father, not some guy playing Army around the world."

Those years had been tough. After the divorce, the wife and daughter moved back to Savannah. He got a one-bedroom apartment in Fayetteville, North Carolina and focused on work. He didn't leave the Army until he was 54 years old, and they kicked him out.

When he first enlisted, his platoon sergeant told him the Army is like an abusive husband: no matter how much you loved Big-Green she would never love you back. Back then it seemed silly, now it seemed prophetic.

"I hear that, brother. Your ex needed support. Now my ex was a bit different, she needed dick. So, when my dick was halfway around the world, she found a replacement," Joe said.

"Well, I guess you can't fault a woman for knowing what she needs."

"It's like oxygen, or food. Some people just need certain things to survive. My ex-wife needed cock. I came home from an 8-month deployment to a 6-month pregnant wife. Plus, I was a shitty husband, so there's that," Joe's smile got even bigger.

"You ever have any kids?" Neil asked as he scanned the road for any hidden dangers.

"Not that I know of, which is weird since the ex-wife kept getting pregnant."

"Fuckin A."

Through Baghdad's dusty brown haze, he saw traffic was slowing.

"Looks like an overpass collapsed," the lead driver called.

"Go around on the shoulder."

The caravan moved on. The lead truck was careful to avoid the likely hiding places for bombs, trash piles and such. Arriving at the collapse the team observed chaos. A car bomb had gone off.

Snap, Snap, Snap.

Rounds started hitting the Suburbans.

Joe looked up and saw a group at the top of the embankment near the overpass.

"Someone wants to make new friends," Joe said.

"You think it's about 400 meters to our new amigos?"

"Bout' right."

"Radio the Army and let them know what's going on. Ask not what your country can do for you, ask who you can shoot in the face for your country."

The *brrrp, brrrp, brrrp* of the team's machine guns started. The air-pressure shifted as the bullets went out.

"Something stirring 50 yards out, by the broken concrete," squawked the radio.

Neil saw a little girl, about 5 years old. She was sitting in between two chunks of concrete. Her face was blank and dusty. There was a blue bow in her brown hair and her dark eyes were puffy. She was rocking back and forth. A woman in a burqa was next to her. The burqa was dark and covered in blood. The woman was probably mom and looked dead.

Bullets cracked past. His ears started to get that muffled full-of-cotton sensation. The edges of his vision blurred. The hair on his one good arm stood up.

"It's a God-Damned little girl," Joe said.

"How about you call for some suppressive fire?" Neil asked.

"We're hitting the road in about 2 minutes. Already told Uncle Sugar bout this goat-rope."

"Hold off, maybe I can save a kid, seems like a good way to spend the morning."

"Cut out this white-savior bullshit. This isn't the Peace Corps, and you aren't a rich girl on Instagram. We got no one to impress, and haji's aimed in."

"Squirt a few rounds up there, get'em to drop their heads. I got this."

"Fuck it, cowboy up," Joe replied. He looked at the debris strewn 40-yard distance to the child.

"Hold my rifle, faster with just the pistol."

Joe called across the radio, "When I start sending rounds

let's help some assholes meet some virgins. Neil is going to extract that kid. We're providing suppressive fire."

Neil focused on the child and then turned to watch Joe. Joe's right thumb moved his weapon's selector from safe to semi, he took aim, the pad of his right index finger pressed the trigger, the trigger released the hammer, striking the pin, exploding the primer, igniting the powder, and launching the 90-grain bullet at 3000 feet per second.

Recoil pulsed into Joe's shoulder. On the embankment was a quick flash of red. The round had impacted his right cheek to the side of the nostril.

"Fuck that guy extra."

The team started firing machine guns in controlled 5 round bursts.

Neil ran. Inbound AK-47 rounds sounded like hollow pops. The return fire sounded sharper, crisper.

Half-century-old knees slowed him. He focused three feet ahead, a fall and the enemy would put a round in his neck.

Sliding behind the larger of the chunks he stopped next to the girl.

Next to the kid lay the woman in a pool of blood. To the other side was a boy wearing a red "Atlanta Falcons 1998 Super Bowl Champions" t-shirt. His right leg was gone. He had bled out. He crawled over, grabbed the girl, and put her over his shoulder. She didn't resist.

The gun smoke was thick.

He thought about all the good men that died. He knew he didn't deserve to live.

"Cover me while I move!"

The sprint back was brutal. His legs were heavy, lungs on fire.

10 yards out lightning shot up his right leg. He fell, sliding face first in the dirt, stopping 4 yards from his team. A

small mound of dirt protecting him and the girl from in-coming bullets.

"You ok?" Joe called.

"I'm good." Neil looked down—a bullet had hit his Achilles tendon. His right foot was useless. Why the hell was it always his right side?

"Haji's tracking you."

"No shit. I need you to kill them."

The tendon made it impossible to carry the girl and run. He saw the medic's outstretched arms.

"Catch the kid."

"Throw the kid and haji will know what's what. You'll catch a round as soon as you move. You need to go at the same time," Joe said over the roar of the fire-fight.

"Together is too slow. She flies, I run. Get ready to catch."

"You sure?"

"Yup."

"Fuckin-A."

Neil grabbed the girl and launched her across the gap. The medic caught the child. The enemy saw her fly and focused on the gap.

"She good?"

"Golden."

"Ramp up that suppressive fire, I'm coming."

Fresh adrenaline exploded in his veins. He gritted his teeth and accepted the pain. He jumped to his feet, pushed off his good left foot, and ran towards the team.

His right side erupted. White-hot pain overtook his mind, then left. He felt peace. In some distant place. He remembered that the protective vest didn't cover his sides. But that was ok. He felt calm.

The darkness came. It was peaceful and still and it was all finally over.

Slowly he became aware. He could hear, but not see. It was muffled, calm.

"Where am I?"

"You died in an honorable way, you are in heaven, Valhalla."

"It was real?"

"All of it, my son, welcome to paradise. Your reward."

"What do I do now?"

"First you accept your lord and savior."

Neil tried to open his eyes.

"It is ok child, you do not need to see. Now when you are ready… cowboy-up and stop being a little bitch."

"What?"

"We got you to the smart-kids fast. Stitched you up good. Quit playin hurt!" Joe said. He punched Neal in the non-shot arm.

The last thing Neil heard was Joe inviting a nurse for a drink in the green zone.

THE PALM GROVE

THE PLINK-PLINK SOUND would not stop, and Clint thought it could be a mechanical issue. He got on the radio and asked if anyone else heard it.

"That's small arms fire hitting the side of the Bradley. Some dumb motherfucker's trying to kill us," was Ram's muffled response.

They had been shot at during foot patrols. Sometimes people screwed with them when they were in their lighter vehicles. However, until now no one was ever stupid enough to attack a Bradley, basically a mini-tank, with a rifle. The unit was transporting food in the backs of the Bradleys to another unit stationed at a combat outpost, or CP. The CP had not eaten fresh food in two weeks. Clint had even brought a mess sergeant to serve the men. He thought the incoming fire must be a mistake, but this was his first deployment and Ram's third, so he didn't argue.

Calling down through the opening in the turret of the Bradley, Clint asked, "Ram, how many months total have you spent in Iraq?"

"Total, about 30, LT and 9 months in Afghanistan."

Clint considered the number. It was his first deployment, and they were only a few months in. When he was a sophomore at The Citadel learning Spanish Ram was on the thunder run from Kuwait into Baghdad. It was hard to be a 23-year-old officer and be the leader of a large group of experienced vets. The way they said "LT" and "Sir" came out like a curse word.

"Why the hell would someone attack a Bradley with small-arms?" Clint asked as he blew a wad of dust from his nose. The free passage of dry air brought the smell of diesel and sweat.

"Well Lieutenant Harvat, Sir, they're probably trying to suck us into an ambush or some other terrorist bullshit. I bet that road has more IEDs than my ex-wife had boyfriends... and she had a lot of boyfriends. She was a whore. Or I guess a slut since she never got paid."

"It is a well-defined distinction, Sergeant Ramirez."

"Fucking-A, and call me Ram, Sir. You got a girl?"

"I got an ex. Let's just say she never got paid either."

They had been engaged and Clint had been sure she was "the one". She cheated on him 3 months into his 12-month deployment. At least she had the decency to tell him the truth and not string him along. Also, since they weren't married and had no kids, she wouldn't be getting half his money. Compared to most of the guys in his unit that was a successful relationship. The whole thing still twisted his stomach. Three years of commitment down the drain. All he had to go back to was a one-bedroom apartment in a depressing army town. Well, things could always be worse; at least he didn't have to deal with child support. Time to re-focus, some assholes are shooting at him. Should he ignore the small arms fire or deal with it? On the one hand, a rifle attacking a Bradley was a waste of time, effort, and bullets. On the other hand, if he was in a soft-sided vehicle or if the terrorist shot at some idiot that would drive down the adjacent dirt road in pursuit... Then some good guys could get killed.

"All units this is Panther 5, hold up," Clint called across the radio. The 4 tan Bradley fighting vehicles under his command came to a halt. The Bradley's firepower was formidable. It consisted of a turret-mounted Bushmaster cannon, a coaxially attached 7.62-millimeter machine gun, a rarely used TOW missile launcher, and a rear passenger area with a 6 man fire-team of pissed-off infantry Soldiers all armed with an M4 carbine. Running the vehicle was a crew consisting of the driver, gunner, and commander. It was hot in the Bradley. The 40 pounds of body armor they wore didn't help. Every night he prayed for air-conditioning, but the prayer was never answered. It ran about 130 degrees in the passenger compartments.

Pulling off his helmet Clint looked at Ram. He looked like your stereotypical All-American, blonde hair, blue eyes, fair skin. The fact that his name was as Latino as possible was an endless source of entertainment for the guys. Clint didn't mess with him because he felt the need to keep the relationship professional. It was hard enough earning the men's respect.

"Ram, by the way, I have been meaning to ask you. You are from the Tennessee mountains, right?"

"Damn straight, Rocky-Top for life."

"Where did you get your name?"

"Well, sir, that's a damn fine question. You see, believe it or not, I am what some people might call a red-neck." Ram said.

"You don't say."

"I do, and I know, it's shocking. Well, you see, my great grandpa was from Spain and went by Marcos Manuel Ramirez. He came to Johnson City for the cheap land. However, despite the cheap land, it is internationally known that the mountains of Tennessee are the most beautiful place in the world."

"Obviously."

"Believe it or not, pig farming in Spain is about the same as pig farming in Johnson City. So great grandpa stuck around and married a local girl. Johnson City has some of the most gorgeous women in America of course. He named his son, my grandpa, Marcos Manuel Ramirez Junior. Dad was Marcos Manuel Ramirez the third. So now here I am Marcos Manuel Ramirez number the fourth. With that said, I don't want people thinking I am Mexican. So, I tell everyone to call me Ram. Now, just to be clear, I like the Mexicans. They make good food, work hard, are friendly, and like to drink beer. If I was Mexican, I would be proud to be Mexican, and I would be a damn fine Mexican, but I ain't Mexican. I am from Johnson City and that's by way of Spain. So that's why people call me Ram. Because of pig farms, Mexicans, a beautiful mountain girl, and my love of America, Sir."

"Oldest story in the book." Clint said, "All right, Sergeant Ram. Let's squirt some 7.62 on in there. See if we can make those assholes change their minds about shooting at us."

"You trying to give me a kill-boner over here, Sir?" Ram asked.

"Kill-boner?"

"You don't know about the ole kill-boner? They don't teach you new LTs shit. When you are in a good gunfight you get your heart really going hard, feels like it is going to beat out of your chest. You start getting excited. The bullets are flying, and shit's getting real. All of a sudden you reach down, and you are hard enough to cut diamonds. You know, a kill-boner."

"You're a sick guy, Ram. You need to see the shrink when we get back stateside."

"It's natural, a beautiful thing sir," Ram said as a big smile flashed across his face, a brown line of Copenhagen chewing tobacco trickling down his chin.

"All elements this is Able 5, if you are taking rounds respond with your machine gun, try to identify your target," Clint called over the radio. Immediately the guns opened up.

The incoming rounds increased in frequency. Clint thought it sounded like rain on a tin roof.

"Well Sergeant Ram, that seemed to have pissed them off," Clint said.

"You just can't teach some people. I guess the A-rabs don't understand that they are messing with the U.S. of A. What are you thinking sir?"

"I am going to pop on the radio, see if we have any air support."

"Pop on over there, LT."

"Dakota 362, Dakota 362, this is Able 5," Clint said.

"Able 5 this is Dakota, go ahead with your traffic."

"Dakota we are taking some rounds on Route Tampa, just south of Mahudiyah. The rounds are coming from a palm grove to the east. We got 4 Bradleys on the ground.

"Able 5, I am en-route. I will do a quick flyby and let you know what's shaking."

Clint heard the helicopters fly overhead and realized the infantry was a poor career choice and had been for about 4000 years.

"Able 5, this is Dakota 362. We got a few military-age males with rifles shooting at you. There are a bunch of women and kids hanging out as well."

"Time to earn those big bucks LT," Ram said.

"All Able elements, this is 5. Return fire," Clint said on the radio.

He hoped that the machine guns would stop the incoming rifle rounds, but they kept on.

"Dakota 362, this is Able 5. Can you do a low and fast flyover of that grove? Let them know we got an Apache on location. Hopefully that will spook them."

The Apache fly-over didn't slow down the incoming rounds. Clint realized he was going to have to move into the village. If he didn't take care of the problem a soft friendly unit could get hurt.

"Dakota this is Able 5, what kind of loadout do you have?"

"We got rockets, you want us to fire some in there?"

Clint looked over and asked, "What do you think Sergeant Ram?"

"Well, lots of women and kids in there. That's a tough decision… You ever shot at a kid before, Sir?"

"I can't say I have."

"I shot a woman holding a baby once. She was pointing an AK47 at me. It was the definition of them or me. But I still can't sleep. It's a hard thing. That's why God gave us whiskey. Sleep is for pussies anyway."

Clint realized he owed it to his men to stop the threat. His feelings didn't matter. He took a deep breath and got back on the radio.

"Dakota this is Able 5, fire the rockets in there."

"Able 5 this is Dakota, I need your initials for the logs. Need to know who is firing these rockets."

"JB, Lieutenant Clint Harvat."

As soon as he transmitted his name Clint heard a loud whoosh. He couldn't tell how many had been fired. Whoever was shooting at Clint's unit stopped.

"All units this is 5, we are going to roll into there and see what's-what. I am calling in explosive ordnance disposal just in case. So, if you see anything weird just make a note of it and steer clear," Clint called on the radio.

The Bradleys made it about 100 yards from the palm grove when the road became too narrow to move forward. There were canals on both sides of the road, and it smelled like rotten fish. There were dust-covered palm trees lining the way. The route turned slightly to the left and disappeared behind the vegetation.

"Able 5 this is Dakota. I am not seeing any more movement on your sight. Looks like you got a little water-well with a mud wall around it and three houses around that. The far house has a livestock pen. Looks like the bad guys are down. A bunch of other people scattered and ran off through the back fields. I am going back to refuel and reload. Stay safe." Through the dust Clint watched the Apache fly towards Bagdad. Anytime things started getting interesting they had to re-fuel.

Clint got on the radio and said, "All right everyone let's dismount and move forward on foot. Drivers and gunners stay with the vehicles and man the turrets. Be ready to provide suppressive fire."

The ramps lowered on the back of the Bradleys. The soldiers exited and moved into staggered formation, called a squad column. The column was constructed of an even smaller v formation called a fire team wedge. Sergeant Ram was the leader of the first wedge. The men moved out the back of the Bradleys like angry bees streaming out of a hive. They wore dark Oakley sunglasses, Kevlar helmets, and bulky body armor all in digital green camouflage. The troops left about 10 yards between each man so that if one of them stepped on an explosive it wouldn't kill multiple people. After Lieutenant Harvat found his position at the middle of the formation they started moving forward slowly. It was about 200 yards from the safety of the Bradleys to the now smoking hamlet.

"We are going to move in and see if we can identify who was shooting at us. I already radioed back to the commander. He is tracking, we should have artillery support. The medevac choppers are up in case things go south. Explosive ordinance disposal is on the way. Let's move," Clint called out.

With each step, small plumes of dust shot up. The air felt gritty in their mouth and filtered the sunlight. Everything looked like an old sepia photograph. The men, no women served in the unit, kept their heads rotating back and forth looking for danger. They were young, most not yet of legal drinking age, and eager for a fight. They came from small towns and squalid inner cities.

As they arrived at the edge of the hamlet, they could see three small homes made out of mud and straw bricks, all topped with rusted tin roofs. Stray dogs started barking as soon as they got close. The streets were dirt and three dead bodies, a man with a rifle and a woman clutching a teenage girl, lay bloody and unmoving.

"Everyone hold up, take a knee. Let's go slow, look, listen, and smell. Make sure we aren't walking into some shit." Clint called out over his handheld radio, stopping their movement.

"Sgt. Ram, this is Able 5, see anything weird?"

"5 this is Ram, negative, looks like most everyone cleared out when the rockets started. They have a way of making people re-think their bad choices. I only see three probable dead Hajis."

"All elements, this is 5, remember-" that is when he heard the ring of a cell phone. There was a flash of light and heat. He felt a pressure wave pass through his chest cavity. He lost his hearing, and the edges of his vision went dark. He saw his men scrambling and the machine guns started firing.

Across the radio he faintly heard, "This is Ram on point, we got contact to the front, two hundred meters. Bomb just went off. We got incoming rounds"

"All elements, this is 5, react to ambush."

With that his men moved to find any cover they could. The air smelled like cordite and time seemed slow. The sepia palate never changed. Clint dove behind the small wall protecting the well. Looking to his left and right he saw two of the junior enlisted men of his unit, buck privates. One, a young black kid whose nametag said Smith, had a huge smile. The other, a white kid with blonde hair named Gerry, looked about as calm as a man walking to get his haircut. He could hear bullets hitting the other side of the wall and saw them splashing into the dirt around him.

"Y'all good?" Clint asked.

"Fuck yea, remember what Patton said in that movie LT. Don't die for your country. Make that other asshole die for his!" Smith said, as he leaned around the wall and fired a string of shots.

"Didn't come here to make friends," Gerry said. With that Smith shouted "Reloading" and simultaneously Gerry leaned around the wall and started firing. Hot brass casings were everywhere.

"You guys hold it down here. I am going to move east to that shack. Looks like a bunch of our guys are over there." Clint said and with the next reload he ran the 10 feet to the mudbrick shanty protecting about 9 of his men. Bullets hit the ground as he ran.

"What's up boys?" Clint asked.

"I am a God-Damned cook! Why the fuck am I being shot at!" Mess Sergeant Thomas screamed.

"Well, Sergeant, if you play stupid games, you win stupid prizes," Clint said as he flashed a grin at the other men.

"Fuck this, Sir," was Thomas's response.

Clint looked around and thought about the assets he had on hand. He was behind the shack on the west side of the hamlet with 9 men. Two of his men were behind the wall in the center of the courtyard. Slightly in front of him and to the east he saw Sergeant Ram and 10 more men, including his medic. They were taking rounds from the front. The explosion didn't seem to have injured anyone.

"All elements this is 5. Can we get a positive ID on where the inbound fire is coming from? All squad leaders give me an all-clear on your men. We need to know if anyone got fucked up."

"Clear" came from all 3 of the squad leaders. None of his men had been injured. Clint let out a sigh of relief.

"It's coming out of that house behind the cow pen." Was the response from someone on the radio.

"First squad, lay down suppressive fire, get those guns talking. Conserve your ammo. Sergeant Ram, keep that shit in line. Second and third squads, you're with me. We are going to loop around this building and hit the west side of that house behind the cow pen. You two jokers stuck in the middle of the courtyard, don't get shot. You guys back with the Bradleys, let me get my driver to prepare a medevac order, gunner see if we can get more air support, and get our fire direction officer on board, tell me what kind of artillery we have available. Ram, in 10 seconds squirt a good long burst with that machine gun. Get those terrorist assholes to put their heads down."

Soon approximately 65 rounds of 7.62-millimeter bullets exploded from first squad's position.

"Able 5, this is your gunner. Air support is 10 minutes out. I got the 9-line medevac report pulled up should we need it, negative on the artillery, they are supporting some Marines that are getting fucked up down in Haswa."

"Sounds good, we're moving. When I throw my grenade all suppressive fire elements shift fire to the eastern-most wall of that compound."

Clint got up and started running with his men close behind. He noticed that the outgoing muzzle flashes continued to focus on the support team, his assaulting element was advancing unnoticed. They quickly looped behind a destroyed cottage and stopped at a mud hut just to the side of the target house. A sergeant took each side of the wall with their men lined up behind them.

Clint mentally rehearsed the procedure for using a fragmentation grenade and took a deep breath. He reached down onto his load bearing equipment and pulled out the M67. He did a quick peek around the corner to get an idea of his target and saw a small window 50 feet away. He would aim for the window, but if he missed the building would make sure the blast didn't come back on his men.

Holding the lever tight he pulled the pin. Breathing in through his nose he stepped out and launched the grenade. He stepped back behind cover before he saw if it made the window. After about 5 seconds he heard a loud explosion and he saw the bullets from his support team shift to the far side of the building.

"Assault team we are going to bound up to the house and clear it out. It looks like a one-room single story deal."

The men flowed around the building and to the target. They had to step over a skinny cow that had been torn to shreds by their bullets. They quickly entered the room. Clint called "Ceasefire" across the radio and the support team stopped their shooting.

Once in the room they saw their shooter, it was a boy, he looked about 14. His right leg was blown off by the grenade and his torso had multiple gunshot wounds. A dirty Thwab, or Iraqi man dress, was all he was wearing. He was lying face down and the blood was pooling near his outstretched right hand.

The room had almost no furniture. The owner was poor even for a warzone. The assault team went through and made sure no one was hiding behind the threadbare blue corduroy couch or in the bathroom. After they determined the house was clear Clint got back on the radio and had everyone check themselves for any injuries.

"All elements, this is Able 5 we are clear in the house. Gunner, call back and get me some Iraqi police out here to take care of this mess. Also, see if the boss wants to send one of those evidence-gathering teams out here. Squad leaders give me a sitrep. Let me know if anyone is hurt, our ammo, and our water levels."

One by one the squad leaders came to Clint and let him know that they were all good. The support team came up. The junior Soldiers set up a perimeter while Sergeant Ram and Lieutenant Harvat sat inside the courtyard, the shooter's dead body was in Harvat's line of sight.

"Everyone, this is Ram," came across the radio. "None of you fuck-sticks touch this body. These Hajis love to booby trap themselves. We are sitting our happy asses here and waiting for the explosive ordnance disposal jokers."

Clint looked down and saw that his hands were shaking. His hearing was slowly coming back. He looked to his left, and he saw the mess sergeant softly crying. Turning to his right he saw a seated Sergeant Ram. This was the first time he had killed anyone. He didn't know what he should feel. He thought that it would be different, that he would have some kind of clarity, but he felt the same.

Sergeant Ram looked at Clint with a huge grin and spit a line of brown tobacco juice into the dust. "God damn sir! You look worried as shit! Don't you know none of this matters? We're all just leather meat bags, out here running around the desert so some politicians can get a few extra dollars. Don't you worry about those dead Hajis, that don't mean shit. Ain't your fault he decided to pick a fight with a bunch of bad-ass mother-fuckers!"

Clint looked at Ram and gave his most enthusiastic fake smile.

A THERAPEUTIC DEATH

THE
BUNKER

FORWARD OPERATING BASE Rusty was a series of undulating earth-tones and temporary buildings coated in grit. The dust made its way between a person's teeth. The Iraq dirt smelled worse than back home.

Captain Bart Eldridge was tired of it. He was exhausted. Ever since his girl sent him the Dear John email the world seemed played out.

Bart had been in Iraq for eight months. He didn't have anything or anyone waiting. Baghdad was home now, mentally. He still wanted to go other places… but it felt like planning a vacation.

Mom still emailed, but her tone had evolved. When you're gone for so long people adapt. Bart knew he'd faded from everyone's consciousness. Iraq owned him.

He thought more about the email. The message was short, and it hurt. She was from Panama… A Dear Juan situation.

The mortar attacks hit daily. Local crowds provided cover for the assaults. The terrorists avoided nighttime. The Army's sighting technology was too advanced, and the streets were empty. Darkness belonged to the Americans. It was for patrols and getting shot at. The grind. He never saw who pulled the trigger or got to return fire.

It was Bart's entire life, existing in the beige, trying not to die, knowing it didn't matter. Sometimes he hoped the next attack had better aim. But then he felt guilty. It would crush mom.

One of his men, L.B., got it. He killed himself with a machine gun. Bart thought that was interesting. Not many people shoot themselves three times. They named a chow-hall after him, the food there sucked.

Bart gathered up his team to get ready for the night's presence patrol. They met just after sundown, it was cold. Bart loathed presence patrols. Simply existing in a place was all they were good for. When one of them died it made the whole thing unbearable.

They left the gate and Bart waited for his heart rate to kick up, the adrenaline surge. But it never arrived. The rush stopped a few weeks back.

They turned north on Route Tampa towards Baghdad and rolled for an hour before the first hit.

"We got a pop, small one, upfront, Captain," the lead driver said across the radio. Bart heard Alabama's song Dixieland Delight playing softly in the background and someone in the vehicle was talking about sending money back to Savannah for a stripper's rent.

"Got it," Bart said. "It fuck-up the truck?"

"Nope."

"You still mobile?"

"Yup."

"Drive."

"These jabronis fucking suck at being terrorists."

"Just go."

Bart never had his guys halt for the small ones. The locals put them out as a distraction. Then when they get out to check out the damage, the terrorists jam home the big one. It happened a few months back. None of his people were hurt. It was luck, not leadership.

They rolled through empty streets and past shot-up buildings. No one was out. Bart sipped Coca-Cola and ate peanuts. It reminded him of his old home. He used chewing tobacco, Copenhagen snuff. It was nasty and he hated it and he knew he should feel bad, but he didn't give a shit.

An hour later got slapped with another little IED. No damage. They got back to the combat outpost around the time bars close. L.B.'s chow hall was supposed to be open, but it wasn't.

The lack of food made his men grumpy. Bart didn't care. He went to his little trailer and got in bed dirty.

The sun started to break on the horizon. A sliver of fire through the brown haze. He sat up, packed his tobacco, and turned on a cheesy horror movie, 1408. The movie was scary. Horror movies always fucked him up.

A movie clown jumped. Bart screamed and threw his laptop and broke it and a propane tank topped rocket hit outside and made a terrific explosion. He felt scared and it was nice.

He thought about waiting the violence out, but his hosing unit wasn't protected. Only senior officers received that luxury. Bart's life was less valuable.

Mom and his Soldiers came to mind. Bart ran to the cement bunker. He baseball-slid inside and his leg opened up. It stung in a far-off kind of way.

An explosion rattled the space. Little concrete flecks floated down and got in his nose and eyes. Sergeant Ramirez, Ram, was already there, smoking a Camel. Some old-school David Allen Coe played from a little handheld device next to him. Ram smiled from ear to ear. His teeth were yellow.

Ram was fair-skinned and light-haired and red-necked. He was objectively big and amazingly average in appearance. He hailed from the Tennessee Mountains, Johnson City. His great-great grandpa was a pig-farmer from Spain who immigrated and became a pig farmer in Tennessee. He preferred 'Ram' to his Latin-sounding given name. Ram gave Bart shit for being a "big-city boy" from Atlanta.

Bart shook as he picked gravel out of his calf.

"You normally don't get so excited," Ram said. "You turning into a little bitch?"

"I was watching 1408."

"The one with Lloyd Dobler?"

"John Cusack. It's the one about the hotel room."

"I've seen it. You watching alone?"

"Yup."

"At daybreak, in Iraq?"

"Correct."

"That a good choice?"

"Guess not."

Ram considered Bart's answer. The music got slower. Ram blew a smoke ring and turned to Bart. "Ready to get back to Fort Benning?"

"Sure," Bart said. "You?"

"Fuck yea, got a new four-wheeler."

"Cool."

"I'm gonna tear it up."

"Nice."

"Four-wheelers are fun."

"I agree."

"I got something good to look forward to."

"Something."

"It's enough."

"Guess so."

"You think too much. You should get a four-wheeler."

"Yea?"

The silence came back. They'd been almost blown-up

together dozens of times and didn't need to fill the space with empty words.

"These rockets are gonna keep coming," Ram said.

"Yea."

"No reason to get upset. Shit's gonna come… these rockets. All you can do is hope you don't catch one and try to have fun in the meantime."

The attack ended and they left the concrete womb. Ram had smiled and talked about drinking cheap beer and riding four-wheelers the entire time.

Bart walked back to his trailer and thought about what was next. He felt different.

THE
MORTAR

SERGEANT CORDOVA FROWNED. "Captain Stevens, you normally don't get so upset by mortars, what's under your skin?"

"I was watching 1408," I responded.

"The horror movie with Mathew Broderick?"

"It was John Cusack, but yes."

"It's based on the Stephen King story?"

"Yes."

"Alone, at night, in Iraq?"

"Yes."

"Can I give you a few life tips… Sir?

"Send em."

"Don't give your ex-wife the keys to your Camaro, don't dismount after getting hit by an unknown attacker, and the most important…"

"What's the most important thing?"

"Don't watch horror movies alone, at night, in Iraq, with all due respect… Sir."

Stevens wasn't sure about the respect.

THE
GEORGIA
QUEEN

HECK AND BACCA met at the Riverside Biergarten, Savannah's best German spot. The place was hip and industrial and smelled of roasted meat and spilled beer. Bacca wanted a smoked bratwurst before the event. Heck got an order of pretzel bites, hoping they would settle his roiling stomach—they did not.

As Heck's brother was rotting in jail for murder... He just couldn't calm down.

Heck lifted a salty brown morsel, looked at it, and put it down. "If things break bad, we meet here. Got it?"

Bacca chewed her sausage with an open mouth. "Got it." Bacca grinned. "Setting rally points, making plans, getting it done. I feel like we're back in the sandbox."

"Yeah, but the war was bullshit. Tonight, we're keeping my brother off death row. This matters."

"Fucking A." Meat flecks sailed out of Bacca's mouth. She slammed a fist on the table. "I miss this vibe. That pre-mission pucker. I feel alive."

"Stay calm, I need you at your best tonight."

"Will do. Show me a picture of Chad again."

Heck pulled up a photo and handed over the phone.

Bacca took it. She looked close. "This is the guy that did it?"

Heck took the phone back. He put it in a plastic bag next to his wallet. "Yup, and we need to prove it."

Bacca nodded.

They walked down the riverfront to the *Georgia Queen*. She groaned in her mooring, backlit by the sunset. Heck smelled the sea. The night was warm, and the air hung moist, comforting Heck. Dampness felt like home. Iraq was dry.

They handed a kid their tickets and walked up the gangplank. Heck put the stub in his pocket. He felt the cellphone and wallet, both inside in a water-proof plastic bag.

It was an 80's night booze-cruise on the *Queen*. The ship reeked of cigarettes and stale beer. The costumed-crowd was packed in, shoulder to shoulder—boisterous and drunk. Heck had lost the paper-rock-scissors competition. He wore the Goose costume. Bacca was Maverick.

Chad's Facebook post said he'd be at the party, but that meant nothing. Heck felt his neck get hot. He needed an item with Chad's fingerprints to prove Chad committed the murder.

They walked inside the ship, clanked up metal stairs, and found spots on the edge of the dance floor.

Heck looked around for Chad but had no luck. He turned to Bacca.

"Put your phone on vibrate," Heck said. "If you see Chad, text me. I'll do the same."

"Sounds good." Bacca nodded along to "Blitzkreig Bop" and flicked her chin at a young woman. "I'm going to hit on that Ghost Buster in about four beers."

Heck frowned. "We're here to work."

"I know, but I hate to waste this hotness." Bacca ran her hands up and down the costume. "I look cool as hell."

"Damnit. You do. How'd you get a real pilot's helmet?"

Bacca flipped up the tinted googles. "I was inverted."

"That makes no sense."

"Doesn't have to." Bacca flipped the lenses down.

Heck laughed.

"Time to buzz the tower." Bacca sauntered to the bar and ordered two beers from a Burt Reynolds, *Smokey and the Bandit*, look-a-like.

Bacca came back and handed over a bottle.

Heck pointed at the bartender. "Wasn't Bandit from the seventies?"

Bacca frowned and strolled to the bar. She leaned in and whispered.

The bartender turned to Heck and shouted. "I'm from the sequel."

Bacca returned and nodded, gravely. "Bartender's story checks out."

"Enough messing around. This is serious. Let's post up, nurse these single beers, and find Chad."

Bacca frowned. "Only one?"

"If I needed a drinking buddy, I would have brought my brother."

"I thought we were here because your brother's in jail."

"You know what I mean... Figuratively... Just don't get wasted."

"Okay."

Bacca stood near the door and watched the entrance. Heck observed the bar and dance floor. They texted back and forth. After two hours, neither had seen Chad. Heck's hair felt like it was standing on end.

A *Tears for Fears* song cut off and the loudspeaker crackled.

"Ladies and Gentlemen, I hope you're ready to party. The staff is pulling the lines. Please drink responsibly."

Heck frowned and glanced at Bacca. Bacca gestured to the gangplank. Heck looked.

A guy dressed as John McClane jogged up. He displayed a ticket in his outstretched right hand. It was Chad.

"Hold the boat," Chad said.

A pimple-faced crewman sighed. "We're leaving, and un-moored. You're late."

Chad frowned. "I got held up at Nakatomi tower."

The crewman shrugged. "Never heard of it."

"Dude," Chad said. "The walkway's still out. Just let me on."

"It's called a gangplank." The crewman waved Chad aboard.

"Sure." Chad grinned. "Yippee-Ki-Yay Motherfucker."

The ship pulled out and chugged down the river, towards the Atlantic. An air horn blared and Heck smelled diesel. They watched Chad.

Once they were clear of the river and entering the ocean, a loudspeaker popped and the Captain came across. "Welcome to 80's night on the *Queen*. Sit back, have a Bartles & Jaymes, and groove to Bon Jovi. Party on and vogue it up."

Bacca texted Heck. "Now what?"

Heck answered. "Take turns getting close, grab anything that holds fingerprints. I'll go first. When I break off, you step in. Don't get noticed."

Bacca looked at Heck and winked. Heck shimmied his hips.

An hour passed. Chad was an enthusiastic dancer and a heavy drinker. He often went to the restroom and returned rubbing his nose. Heck noticed a trickle of nasal blood. Chad seemed to be alone. Unfortunately, Chad didn't litter. Every bottle of Corona he finished, he put straight into the trash can. Heck wasn't comfortable going dumpster diving on a crowded boat. It would make a scene and Chad might notice.

A THERAPEUTIC DEATH

Heck had to get a copy of those fingerprints, or his brother was looking at life in prison.

The buffet opened. The scent of cheap fried chicken drifted out. Multicolored strobe lights flashed. Heck and Bacca nursed their single beers and hunted for an opening.

Heck texted Bacca. "One of us should dance. We look creepy."

Bacca walked over, leaned into Heck's ear, and gestured to the floor. "I thought we were here to do a job?"

"We are, but we can't look like leering weirdos." Heck said.

Bacca grimaced. "Are you dancing?"

"No. You are."

"What the hell, why me?"

"I have a plan."

"What?"

"I'm going to sneak around to Chad's blind side," Heck said. "I'll see if I can snag a beer bottle. You take the front, the dance floor."

"Fuck you." Bacca frowned. "Can I dance alone?"

"With a partner is less weird."

Bacca took a real drink from his warm beer. "You want me to hit on a girl?"

"Or a guy, one of the two."

Bacca set her jaw. "Screw it." She slid right, towards a young woman dressed as Cyndi Lauper. They shook hands. Heck slinked around the back, close to Chad.

Heck got close. He listened as Chad, overloud, talked at a bored looking Madonna. Chad yapped a mile a minute. He spilled Corona. The woman left. Heck stayed close.

Chad milled about the edge of the dancefloor, pressing upon women. He talked about how much of a "baller" he was and made a general annoyance of himself.

Chad was not getting anywhere with the ladies, and not leaving behind any items.

Heck looked for Bacca. Bacca was kissing Cyndi Lauper and oblivious to the world.

Heck texted, "Get on the dance floor."

Bacca didn't answer.

Two hours passed. Chad yapped. People started giving him a wide berth. Bacca held Cyndi. Heck observed and listened. The Captain came across the sound system. "Time to head back."

Heck hunted for an opening. He heard a yell from across the dance floor.

Heck looked. A mountain of man, dressed as Ivan Drago, loomed over Bacca and Cyndi Lauper. Ivan looked like a former pro-wrestler turned competitive eater—cosplaying a boxer.

"The hell you think you're doing?" The mountain's voice was slurred and deep. He held a barely visible beer in each massive hand. Red gloves were strung together and hanging around his neck.

"Dancing with my friend." Bacca nodded at Cyndi. "What about you, tiny?"

"She's my girl," the mountain said.

Bacca smirked. "She know that?"

The mountain pushed Bacca. Bacca slid backwards, but didn't fall. Baca flipped up her visor and said, "I'm a woman."

The mountain clomped forward. "I don't give a shit." He reached out and pulled Cyndi's arm. Cyndi's face turned red. They had a hushed conversation. The mountain turned to Bacca.

"She tells me you forced her to dance, and you got handsy," the mountain said.

Bacca wagged a finger. "Don't fib, Cyndi. I did no such thing. You were more than willing. Hell, you kissed me."

Bacca pulled out her phone and scrolled through. She showed Drago the screen. "See, she already put her number in here."

The mountain stomped forward and slapped the phone to the ground. The screen shattered. "You calling my girl a liar?"

Bacca looked down, rubbed her chin, and looked up. She squinted. "I am."

The mountain's hips dropped two inches. He rotated his core and drove out his right fist.

Heck called out, "Bacca, duck!"

Bacca didn't duck.

The punch landed clean. Bacca crumpled like a damp towel.

Someone yelled, "That asshole hit a woman."

Someone else yelled, "Maverick is a dude."

A few men stomped towards Drago. Heck threw his beer bottle at the man-mountain. The glass hit Drago's meaty back and fell to the ground.

The crowd stepped away from Heck and pushed in on Drago.

Chad was to Heck's right, three yards away.

The mountain turned. Heck gritted his teeth.

The mountain frowned. "What the hell?"

Heck took a deep breath. "You shouldn't hit women and you never screw with my co-pilot, bitch."

"You're dead." The mountain rumbled forward.

Heck faked right and dipped left. He kicked out his right leg. It impacted the mountain's shins. The mountain yelped and soared forward in a Superman pose.

He fell, face first, and slid on his stomach. He released a deflating-balloon sound. A mass of people started screaming about abusing women.

Heck stood. He acted drunk and disoriented. He stumbled, bumped into Chad, and reached into Chad's pocket.

Heck stole Chad's phone. Heck slipped it into his pants. Chad said nothing and pushed Heck away.

He turned back to the mountain. "We still doing this, Jabroni?"

The mountain got on one elbow. "Fuck you."

Heck rushed forward and jump-straddled the mountain's chest. The man rolled flat. Heck pushed down on the shoulders.

Heck heard a war cry. Cyndi Lauper leapt on his back. She dug her claws in. The bright red fake nails were sharp. Heck jerked his hips up. Cyndi aerial somersaulted forward and landed in a heap. She cursed but didn't move.

The mountain rolled to his stomach and pushed up to all fours. Heck stayed on the mountain's back. Heck put both of his ankles into his opponent's inner thighs, hooked his bent arms under the mountain's armpits, and drove his hips forward.

The big guy went flat onto his stomach. Heck snaked his right hand under the chin, clasped his left bicep, and performed a rear-naked choke.

The big guy clawed at Heck's eyes. "Freedom" by George Michael played. The strangle was fast and the mountain went limp. Heck released. People screamed and snapped photos.

Heck looked right. Bacca was holding his arms out, trying to keep the crowd at bay.

Elton John yelled, "Call the cops."

Marty McFly answered. "Already did. They're waiting for us."

Heck's chest tightened. He looked out, over the railing. They were two hundred meters from the boat's mooring station.

Heck popped up, ran in a circle as if trying to find an exit, and brushed against Bacca. He slipped Chad's phone in Bacca's rear pocket.

Heck sprinted to the stern and jumped overboard. Flashbulbs exploded. "Who Wants to Live Forever" played.

Heck impacted. The water was warm. He went deep.

He stayed under until burning lungs demanded air. He broke the surface. The boat was twenty meters away, electric yellow in the dark night. Heck bobbed in murky water. The river smelled like trash.

Heck swam to Hutchinson Island, across from the mooring station. He clawed up through broken glass and thorny bushes. A frog croaked. He got his bearings and walked to the asphalt.

Just off the road, obscured by trees, he sat and caught his breath, listening for police sirens. After twenty minutes he was confident none were coming. He stretched out and waited for his clothes to dry, no Uber would accept a soaked passenger stinking of river.

Two hours later he was dry and started to think about the way back. His phone pinged and he pulled it from the plastic bag. It was from the Savannah PD detective, the one investigating the murder. "I met with your buddy, Baca. She gave me Chad's phone. The fingerprints match. Your brother's innocent."

Heck's heart rate skyrocketed. "What?"

"You fucking did it."

"My brother is free?"

"Out-processing the jail now."

"Holy shit," Heck said. "Thank you."

"Don't thank me. You did this. Good job."

Heck ordered a ride back to the Biergarten. When he arrived,

Bacca and the Ghost Buster were drinking on a bench next to the store. Bacca held one up for Heck.

Heck took the coffee. "What happened to Cyndi?"

Bacca shrugged. "Cyndi didn't work out. Doesn't matter, I never really got into her music."

Heck laughed. He felt reborn.

A WARTIME BREAKFAST WITH RAMIREZ

AN EXPLOSION JARRED me, and I opened my eyes and knew exactly where I was and there was no confusion. At the beginning of my wartime, when someone tried to shoot me or blow me up, it was disconcerting. After a while, it became a part of life and I almost forgot it is not a normal thing to be almost blown up, but I'd stopped caring. My feelings had stopped working.

I didn't like that they'd left, and I tried to fix it, but nothing had yet worked.

I jumped out of bed, grabbed my M4, put on my dollar store flip-flops, and ran to my grey-concrete bunker. Mine.

Ramirez was already there. He had a deck of cards. While everything blew up we played five-card-draw poker—no betting. It is less fun without gambling, but much cheaper. I usually lose, so this was a best-case scenario.

I pulled out my Skoal wintergreen chewing tobacco and filled the space between my lip and gums with the black shredded leaves. Ramirez gave me shit about the wintergreen again. I told him to stop, but he kept up. The minty smell mixed with the grey dust air. Airborne grit got in my nose and the back of my throat. It made my eyes water.

We talked about women and Ramirez gave me hell about

not having a woman back home. I didn't tell him about the tattoo-face girl I met on the last patrol outside the wire. Soldiers and locals didn't mix, and he wouldn't understand. But, my existence was redundant and I didn't care and she made it less so.

The enemy-fire kept oozing in. Soon, I heard our artillery's outgoing shots. After thirty minutes of back-and-forth-indirect-death-tag, it was over as if it never started and never happened.

When it was done, Ramirez grinned at me. "Breakfast?"

"Yeah," I said. "Let me get dressed."

We went to my housing unit, Ramirez held my rifle and waited outside. Inside, I put on my uniform. My boots fit tighter than normal, and I wondered why. I exited and we went to the chow hall.

The building had been hit by incoming and there was a hole in the north-side corner roof and the north wall. I was glad the hole was far from the hot-chow line, that way no dirt got in my food.

I grabbed a brown-plastic tray and got in line. Quickly, I got to the front. A Bangladeshi food-service contractor gave me scrambled eggs, bacon, pork sausage, a bagel with cream cheese, and pancakes. The food looked great, and I was excited and thankful,

I got a cup of black coffee and a glass of orange juice. The food reminded me of Waffle House back home—I'd went there often with my father and loved the place. I sat down in a blue plastic chair that reminded me of grade school. Ramirez sat across from me, he had just bacon and eggs.

I pointed at his plate. "What's up?"

Ramirez slapped his not-huge-but-noticeable belly. "Going keto."

"Yeah? Why?"

"I got to look good when I get home." He laughed. "Keep the wife from cheating on me."

I laughed. "More, cheating on you more."

Ramirez stopped rubbing his belly. "What do you mean?"

"You know she's getting pounded by some fireman right now."

Ramirez frowned and forced a chuckle. The two Airforce sergeants sitting next to us laughed too loud and guilt bubbled in my gut.

"I'm just playing," I said. "I'm sure she can't want for you to get home and isn't running around or nothing."

Ramirez winked. "Of course, no worries." He looked down and ate his eggs.

My guilt metastasized.

I held up my full coffee-cup. "I'm going to get more, can I get you something?"

"No, I'm good," Ramirez said. "Thanks."

His voice seemed more alive and that made me glad. I didn't want to hurt my friends. I didn't want to hurt anyone.

I walked to the shiny stainless-steel coffee percolator. It was always perfect looking and I wondered if some Bangladeshi guy spent every night cleaning the thing. A guy moves across the world to work for the mighty American war-effort and spends his days wiping fingerprints off a hunk of metal that does nothing other than pour hot-water over crushed beans.

I was a touch jealous, because that seemed like a good and simple and honest existence—maintain a thing that provides happiness to others. Simple and clean and righteous and no moral grey.

Everything I did, every day... Did it make anyone happy? Did my bullshit make anyone's life better? Maybe being the coffee guy is more important than whatever the hell I was.

Since my coffee cup was full, the quest being a ruse, I

poured the dark liquid into a trash can. I refilled my cup. The scent was strong and good. I loved that smell in the morning. I took a sip and it was too hot but tasted great. The food and services were always top shelf at the base, and I appreciated it. I walked to the line and found a Bangladeshi food-service worker.

I made eye contact with the man. "Thank you," I said as I raised my coffee cup.

The worker, who was short and dark-haired, with grey skin, waved and smiled. He was missing a front tooth, and the other was light green. His grin appeared genuine, and I wondered if he was the coffee percolator operator. I wanted to dig into the mystery, but Ramirez hooted so I walked back to the table.

Ramirez's eggs and bacon were gone, as was my bagel.

"I thought you were eating keto," I asked.

Ramirez shrugged. "Every diet needs a cheat day."

"How long you been on the diet?"

"This is my first day," Ramirez said. "Figure I get the cheating out of the way now and it is all smooth sailing."

"Smart."

"If you're gonna be dumb you gotta' be tough."

"I've heard."

"And I'm not tough."

"So you're smart?"

Ramirez tapped his temple with his right index finger. "They're playing checkers and I'm playing chess."

I laughed.

Ramirez pointed left. "That lady came looking for you."

I looked. Bassinette Reeves stood in the corner by the wall-hole. Light from the roof-hole shot down on her like a laser through the dust. She sipped coffee, and I thought of the phantom percolator operator. I stood up and walked over.

She shook my hand and held up her coffee. "You had any of this?"

I felt warm inside, another percolator appreciator. "Yeah."

She turned and threw the cup in the trash. "That's shitty coffee."

My throat got tight. "Sure." Wind rushed through the mortar-hole in the wall and I hoped she would leave soon. "What can I do for you?"

She gestured to an empty table. We walked over and sat.

"I wanted to let you know," Reeves said. "Our investigation into Sergeant Golds' death is complete."

"And?"

She sighed. "It was a freak accident that occurred because he was raising drugged up fighting scorpions."

"Seriously?"

"Yeah. We even brought in an arachnologist from the Smithsonian."

"What's that?"

"The Smithsonian?"

I frowned. "I'm not an idiot, what's an arachnologist?"

"A person with a Ph.D. in bugs. In this case, a specialist in scorpions."

"You brought an insect professor to a warzone?"

"We brought the doctor to Germany—we sent the body to an Air Force base there."

"I guess that makes more sense?"

"The arachnologist did a bunch of tests along with a coroner."

"And?"

"Golds was stung hundreds of times, it overwhelmed his system, and he died." A tear crept out of the corner of Reeves's eye.

"It had nothing to do with the scorpion fights or gambling or money or any of that?"

Reeves looked at him cross-eyed. "You think you're in a John le Carré novel?"

"No," I said. "Why?"

"There's not always some grand design. It's a fucking war."

"So?"

"So people die for stupid reasons, and it is done." More tears came. Reeves stood. "It's a fucking war."

I looked at the lines cutting down her face. "Did you know Golds?"

"I did. We both got here a year ago. I knew him... Well." Reeves turned and walked away. She left through the chow-hall's door—even though the explosion hole was right there and leaving through an explosion hole is a once in a lifetime opportunity.

I thought about the tattoo face girl from the last mission outside the wire and wondered if she was okay and everything was a bit better after thinking of her.

I walked back to the percolator, got another cup, and returned to my table. Ramirez had eaten my pancake and left, so my breakfast was over.

I exited the building through the bomb-hole and went back to my housing. I thought of Reeves's tears and the girl with the blue tattoo lines on her face.

I felt something.

OKEFENOKEE FREEDOM

NO TIME TO worry about getting shot in the back… got to keep moving. This was it. If he got away this time he was done. No more bars, no more meth, no more fast life. He wanted to do the right thing. He was going to make good choices. This time he would try, and he would do it. His messed-up past kept dragging him down. He was the victim in all this. Poisonous people trapped him in bad situations, and he had to make the best of it. All that was over now. Blue was sure, this time.

He knew the Okefenokee swamp was about 15 miles south. If he made it there—he could re-group—figure out the next move.

Damn, what was that sound? Did the guards bring out the dogs? How long would it take to notice he escaped from the Doctor's office? Hope that guard didn't die…

Why the hell would they put one old lady guard on him? It was like they wanted to cause an incident. After taking her out, he put her in that little locked supply closet. It would take a long time for anyone to find the guard. He should have a good head start.

Too many thoughts were running through his mind. He needed to get rid of the noise.

If he stayed to the west of Waycross and kept going south, he would be in the clear. He had looked at a picture on Google Maps. Other than the town, it was all forest and farms until he got to the swamp. Once he was safe, he could rest. First things first, he had to find some clothes. The bright orange jumpsuit with "Prisoner" stenciled on the back wasn't doing him any favors.

Blue kept moving through pines and cotton fields until he came upon a small residential neighborhood off Longwood Road. It was a blue-collar area, which was perfect, because they hung clothes outside to dry.

As he moved, Blue kept thinking about the Judge that had put him away, always talking about the "victims" of crimes. Sure, he had done some illegal stuff, but it wasn't like he was a bad person.

He had a horrible childhood. No one gave him anything, he had to fight and scrape for every single cent his entire life. So what if he got a little messed up on dope and made one bad choice? He deserved to relax every now and then. Of course, he had to pay society for his crimes, but why the hell do they want to treat him like he is 100% at fault?

He was a victim in all this as well.

He felt horrible about how the situation had played out. But no one cared. No one ever tried to see it from his point of view. He made one bad choice, and he was high, so did it even count? He was a decent man; he knew it in his heart.

Blue looked around to make sure no one saw him and took off the prison jumpsuit. He grabbed a well-worn pair of Levi's and a faded grey University of Georgia football shirt from the line. Luckily, they fit his 6-foot 190-pound frame. He was still wearing the tan plastic jail sandals, but hopefully no one would notice those.

Blue walked south through the countryside by Smith

Road. He came up on a small house at the intersection with Valdosta highway and drank some water from the spigot on the side. The heat beat down. The sun was intense here, he had developed a deep tan and light hair from all the time he had spent in the prison exercise yard. He was 35, but could pass for 25 if need be.

"What the hell you think you're doin?" called a female voice with a clipped southern accent.

Blue froze. If his face was on the news he was done. He slowly turned and worked up his best smile. The Reidsville Prison dentist had given him a nice set of pearly whites, replacing what meth had taken.

Standing in the home's sagging doorway was a woman. She looked about 45 years old. Dry wind-swept blond hair. Her skin was red and chapped from too much exposure. She wore washed-out cut-offs and an Allman Brothers t-shirt from their 1975 Jimmy Carter benefit concert. The shirt was full of holes. A cigarette rested in her left hand. 25 extra pounds clung to her midsection. Blue noticed she was not wearing a wedding ring.

"Excuse me ma'am! I am just rude as can be, drinking y'all's water and not asking permission. My name's Steven Goodman, I was walking down Valdosta highway trying to get to town to go apply for a job. I was just about dying of dehydration, it's so dang hot out here. I didn't mean to impose. Let me get out of y'all's hair. Thank you, ma'am." Blue turned and started to walk away.

"Now just hang on a moment there, Mr. Goodman. Jesus was very clear about helping travelers. I ain't the most Christ like, but I'm trying to change that. Why don't you come on inside and have a glass of lemonade and soak up some of the air-conditioning," the woman said.

"Ma'am you are just about the sweetest thing since Coca-Cola," Blue said. "What did you say your name was?"

"Sherry Morefield, but everyone just calls me Cher, like that singer."

"Pleasure to meet you, Cher," Blue held out his hand, Cher accepted. They shook, Blue held on a touch too long. He stared into her eyes. His eyes were light blue, and women loved them. Cher turned red and shifted her gaze.

"Come on inside, Steven, let me get you something cold to drink."

They walked up the rotting wooden stairs into the small yellow home. It looked tired. The floors were beige linoleum. The furniture was dusty, cheap, and beaten down. An off-white wall held photos of presumed family members. There was a framed re-print poster from the stage production of *Legally Blonde*. It was hanging over an ancient cathode ray TV. Cher had Blue sit at a round laminate table surrounded by folding chairs and pulled out a pitcher from the refrigerator.

"You like lemonade?"

"I do," Blue said.

"It's just the powdered stuff, I don't have the time to make fresh squeezed," Cher said.

"I love the powdered stuff," Blue lied.

"Now Mr. Goodman, I don't normally invite strangers into my home. But seeing a grown man drinking water from the side of my house, well I just knew you need some help. I don't want you to think this is a normal thing for me. I am trying to change for the better."

"Let me tell you that you made the right choice. Just seeing you, I could tell you're a good person. I appreciate you looking out for me like this, being a stranger and all."

"You said you were going into Waycross to apply for a job? Do you have any leads?"

"Unfortunately, no. My Momma lives up in Dixie Union. I was there taking care of her. Before that I was living up in Vernal, Utah, working on the oil fields. When Momma got sick, I came back, got here last week. Now I got to find a new job. It's a tough situation without any savings, but a man has to look out for his mother."

Blue looked up at Cher and smiled. She smiled back turning a deep shade of crimson.

"Mr. Goodman—"

"Please, please! Call me Steven."

"Ok, Steven. How's your drink?" she moved into the chair across from him and avoided eye contact.

They sat at the table and talked. His time in prison and hustling on the streets gave him the ability to carry on a conversation with anyone. He was good at telling a person what they wanted to hear, and he was proud of that skill. No one had taught him anything, he had to learn it himself, the hard way. Cher smiled and laughed.

An hour passed, then two. The conversation flowed. Blue had earned her trust. He could tell she hadn't had a man's attention in a long time.

"I hate being so forward, Ms. Cher," Blue said, "but are you married?"

"I don't think that is too forward," Cher said. "It seems an appropriate question being in my kitchen and all. No, I am not."

"Are you seeing anyone?" Blue already knew the answer, but he wanted her to say it.

"No, I'm waiting until I find a respectable man. Until then—I will stay single and happy."

"I understand. It's a struggle to find virtuous people nowadays. I try my best to be an upstanding person. I know I am, in my heart, even if I slip sometimes. I always try to walk in the path of our lord," Blue said.

"I feel the same way. The path of our lord is the only way. I'm glad I met you." Cher said.

He reached out and grabbed her right hand. She didn't pull away. Her hands felt rough and dry. The fingernails were chewed.

"What kind of work are you looking for? Do you know any trades? Maybe I know someone and could point you in the right direction."

"Like I said, I have mostly worked in oil. There isn't a lot of oil drilling around here I imagine."

"No, but a lot of the farmers need wells, so there are drilling jobs. I imagine drilling for water is like drilling for oil?"

"I bet you're right. You're a sharp lady, Cher, a man would be lucky to have you. I hate to ask, but would you mind driving me into town? Maybe I could hunt up a drilling job. Or any job really, I just want to help my mama," Blue said.

"I don't have to be at work for a few more hours, did I tell you I work nights cleaning up at Memorial? I got a bit of time. I can give you a ride."

Cher led the way out of the house, Blue followed. She locked the front door and walked out to the street. She had a patchwork-red late 80's Honda Civic. It looked more rust than metal; the tires were bald. Blue opened the door for Cher, and she beamed back at him.

"It's nice to see there are still some gentlemen left in this world," Cher said.

Blue got in the passenger seat and started thinking about his options. Should he figure out a way to get her to drive to the swamp? Take the car from her? She liked him, that was obvious, maybe he could play up a Robin Hood noble outlaw thing, get her on his side? He had to think fast. If someone asked about drilling, she would see through him in a minute. Next time he is going to have to pick a fake career he knew something about. Maybe a minister—path of Jesus and all that.

They started driving down highway 23 towards Waycross. He could smell the pines and the air was warm. It was good to be free, and he knew he deserved it. As they passed a cop, Blue turned to Cher.

"It's so beautiful today. Do you have a little time before your shift?"

"What are you thinking? Don't you want to look for work?"

"Maybe we could go for a drive and spend time together. I heard there is a beautiful park near here, is that true?"

"The swamp is south of here, but I am not sure if beautiful is the right word. Peaceful maybe?"

"Peaceful sounds just right. How about we look for a job another time. I was looking for a reason to see you tomorrow," Blue flashed his biggest smile.

Cher looked deep into Blue's eyes. Blue was sure that she felt something.

"I was waiting to meet an upright man, and I think you might be him. It's been hard being alone these years."

"I know in my heart I'm a good person, Cher. I've made hard choices, but I'm a man of God. Let's take a ride to that peaceful swamp."

"I'm glad you drank from my faucet… Happy I decided to help a traveler in need."

Cher drove down highway 23. As they got to the entrance of the park, they took a left onto a dirt road that went around the edge of the swamp. After 15 minutes they stopped for an alligator who was sunning himself in the middle of the lane.

"You don't see those in drilling for oil in Utah!" Blue said. "Let's get out and take a look."

"Those things are dangerous," Cher said. "You aren't wearing boots, those jailhouse flip-flops won't protect your feet. We're in the middle of nowhere, let's go back to town. I have work in a bit. We can check out alligators another time. I have a feeling we were meant to find each other." Cher smiled.

"I agree, I think we just might have something happening between us. Wait, did you say jailhouse?"

"Huh? What are you talking about?"

Blue frowned. "Nothing." His throat got tight. "This gator is a treat for me, I'm going to get out." He opened the door.

"Be careful, this swamp is no joke. You never know if something else dangerous is out to get you."

Blue walked toward the animal. The deep vibrant green of the swamp pressed in all around him. He smelled rotting vegetation and heard a cacophony of insects. The alligator snorted and slowly started moving back towards the water.

Cher walked up behind Blue. "You ever seen one before?"

"I haven't."

The gator kept moving right, toward the water. Cher walked behind the animal, keeping her distance.

Blue recognized his opportunity. He hated that he had to do this. Why couldn't she have just left him alone? Why did she have to be so sweet and trusting, agreeing to go to the middle of nowhere with someone she just met, letting him lead her down this path? It was all a damn shame.

He picked up a piece of pine. It was about 4 feet long and as big around as his wrist. As she followed the animal, he slowly walked up behind her. He didn't want to disturb her. It was better if she didn't see what was coming. After all, he didn't want to be cruel.

He took a slight sidestep to the left. His foot landed on a stick—it snapped loudly.

Blue looked up.

A THERAPEUTIC DEATH

Cher turned. She held a gun. "I know those sandals."

There was a boom and a flash. Blue felt heat in his stomach.

He swung the branch, rotating his entire body, and connected with the side of Cher's head. The impact made a hollow thump. Cher fell to her knees, dropped the gun, and she slumped forward onto her face.

Blue raised the smooth piece of pine. He wondered how all the bark had been stripped, and swung it down hard. After 5 swings Cher stopped making noise. A trickle of blood flowed from the back of her head where the skin had split. A small indentation was present in the skull.

After a bit, Cher stopped breathing. Blue grabbed her wrist and didn't feel a pulse. He was glad she hadn't suffered. He reached down and felt his side, her bullet had grazed him and the wound was minor.

He grabbed Cher's ankles and dragged the body along the alligator's trail. Prickly bushes scratched his arms. The sun was high and sweat poured down his forehead.

He felt horrible that he killed the woman, but it had to be done.

At the swamp's edge, Blue dropped her ankles. He reached into her pocket and took out her wallet.

Her ID said "Sherry Morefield—Prison Guard". He pulled out her cellphone. There was a sent text.

"Some idiot with jail slippers is at my door," Cher had typed. "I'm going to bring him in after I take him by the swamp so he doesn't get suspicious."

"Swamp?"

"Yeah, it's a whole thing. Don't worry about it."

"Be safe."

There was a picture of Blue, sitting at Cher's table, included with the message.

As Blue read the text a response came in. "Be Careful.

That perp killed a guard. Do not attempt to apprehend. Call Waycross PD."

Blue pecked out a response. "I'm good, I told him to leave, I'm going to run up to see a friend in Atlanta." He hit send.

Blue frowned. She was lying the whole time. She was fake, and out to get him, and got what she deserved.

He threw the phone into the center of the waterway. He took the car keys. He pushed her body out into the inky black water. The alligators would take care of the rest.

Blue cut back through the long grass and took the gun. He got in the vehicle and headed towards the highway. Once he was out of Georgia, he'd be able to relax. South to Florida, west to Texas. Crossing state lines always slowed the cops. After that, who knows? Mexico? Maybe further South?

As he drove, he thought about all the bull that had caused him to become a criminal. The bad things he'd done, he didn't want to do any of it. But, unfortunately, it had been the only way. He really hadn't wanted to hurt Cher. It was painful. Was he fooling himself…? No, no way.

He was a true victim.

ACKNOWLEDGMENT

Mom and Aunt Kim, thank you.

Alpha and Able companies, you were there for most of this, thank you.

J.B. STEVENS lives in the Southeastern United States with his wife and daughter.

Steven's work in crime fiction is widely lauded. He was a finalist for the Claymore award and won Mystery Tribune's inaugural micro-fiction contest.

Before his writing career, J.B. was a United States Army Infantry Officer and earned a Bronze Star. He is an undefeated Mixed Martial Arts Fighter. He graduated from The Citadel.

Join his newsletter at JB-Stevens.com.

Made in United States
Orlando, FL
22 February 2022